Chapter 1.

Pietre Mortennson stood quietly in the background as
family sped off into the distance. He did not know why he had felt the need to hide behind
one of the old trees flanking the roadside. He just felt that it was the right thing to do – for the
moment at least.

Pietre Mortennson was a good looking young man of 32 who possessed the blonde hair and
clear complexion so typical of Scandinavian people. What he did possess, that was not
necessarily typical, was a deep rooted primeval need for information regarding his heritage.
He had grown up in a small village on the outskirts of Stockholm where he had spent his
entire life. Until a few short months ago he had never considered a life outside of Sweden. As
his thoughts returned, unwillingly, to that moment just a few days after his parents had been
killed his facial expression darkened. How could his parents have lied to him all of his life?
How could they have never told him their secret? As he watched his parents being laid to rest
in the village cemetery he had vowed, there and then, to seek answers. He was an extremely
intelligent young man who had embraced the technology available to him at university. He
had devoured all the knowledge he could and he was thankful for the fact that he possessed
an above average intelligence together with an open mind. His parents had been shocked and
alarmed when he had insisted that he was going to go to University and not become part of
his parent's haulage business. He had never shown any interest in the business and this fact
had alienated him from his Father. His Mother, over the years, had tried unsuccessfully to
encourage him to join the family business and she had never stopped reminding him that he
would be the first person in many generations of the Mortennson family not to be involved.
Could he not see what this was doing to his Father? Did he not realise that everything his
Father had done was to enable his only child to inherit the business?

As Pietre remembered the heated arguments he had endured over the years he felt no sorrow.
He had always felt like an outsider. Oh! His parents had fed and clothed him well enough.
They had encouraged him, at first, in his education but he had always known that they did not
really approve of him. He had always felt that, somehow, he had been a disappointment to
them.

After the funeral Pietre had set about trying to discover his real heritage. He knew that his
parents were fourth generation Swedish but he had had no idea where his great -great
grandparents had originated from.

Over the next few months Pietre had discovered that his ancestors had originated from
Norfolk. He had accessed the records of the Swedish Government and that information had
led him to discover that his lineage had begun.in part, in the little village of Saham Toney.

Pietre made his way slowly away from the large, quietly imposing farmhouse and headed
back to the little bed and breakfast cottage that he had lived in for the last few days.

He had come to the village with little hope of finding any answers but he had been pleasantly surprised by what he had found here. The village church had been a valuable source of local information. He discovered that many families had lived here for generations. He could never quite understand this. He had never felt an affinity to a particular place in his own life. A house was just a house. Wasn't it?

He had no regrets when selling the family run business. He had not had any qualms in handing over the business to his Father's biggest rival. What did he care that his family had always struggled in the face of such stiff opposition? He had always wondered why his Father had never agreed to sell to the Hendrickson Corporation. They had offered ridiculous amounts of money over the years in order to gain acquisition of his Fathers land and business contacts. What was his Fathers problem? If the stupid man had just sold it to them than maybe he would still be alive today! His Father had been incandescent with rage when Pietre had suggested that they take up the ridiculous offer that had come from Gregor Hendrickson just three weeks before his Parents death in a road accident. He would never understand why his Father hated Hendrickson so much.

Pietre Mortennson was a wealthy young man, free from any emotional ties to Stockholm or to Sweden. He did not know where his life was taking him but one thing he did know with absolute certainty was that he would never again go back to living in the quiet village he had grown up in. The place suffocated him in a way that he found hard to describe. The people there had no ambition! They seemed happy with their lot .How could they be happy living the same mundane boring way they had always lived? That way of life was alien to Pietre. He had always wanted to escape and now that he had he was determined to make the best of himself. No more clocking in at the factory for him. He was going to enjoy his new found wealth if it was the last thing he did!

So why did he feel so unsettled? Why was he not dancing in the street?

As he walked back to his room at the cottage Pietre thought about the old lady he had spoken to in the church that day. Maud Carrington had introduced herself to him and had told him that she was in the church with the vicar that fateful evening when some crazy man had stumbled into church in a terrible state. Pietre had discovered that the man, Gordon Jarvis, had escaped from the clutches of some psychopathic ex-soldier who had seemed hell bent on murdering him and several other members of the Carrington family.

For the last few days Pietre had busied himself with trying to discover just who his ancestors were and what was their connection to the village.

He had arranged with Maud, as she insisted he called her, to meet her at the church that afternoon. Maud had telephoned him that morning to say that she might be a little late for their appointment as her daughter and her family were leaving for a vacation in Paris and she simply must be there to see them off!

Maud had mentioned that her daughter and her Cosmetic Surgeon husband, together with her two teenage grandchildren, lived in a large farmhouse on the outskirts of the village.

She told him that the farmhouse was over 200 years old and was absolutely delightful. He must come and look around it before he left. She was sure that her daughter wouldn't mind.

When he had heard this Pietre experienced something quite new to him. He had never thought much about deja-vu before but he had the curious feeling that, somehow, the farmhouse was calling to him!

Even now, some days later, Pietre could not quite shake off the feeling that, somehow, his family was connected to the house. He had not spoken of this to anyone and he had in fact told himself not to be so bloody stupid! Why should he feel like this? What the hell was happening to him? He had decided that he would not go to the farmhouse after all. He would make up some excuse to Maud.

So why was he skulking around outside? Why was he even here?

Pietre Mortennson did not have the answers. All he did know was that he felt compelled to go to the house and try to find out about his ancestors.

Pietre wrapped his scarf more tightly around his face and went, slowly, back towards the front door. No turning back now he thought as his hand reached for the doorbell!

Maud Carrington answered the door and stood staring at Pietre for several seconds before the smile of recognition swept across her face. She apologised profusely for leaving him standing there. What must he think of her? She told him that her daughter and family had just left for their trip to Paris. Had she mentioned that to him? She felt sure that she must have done because they were so excited about the trip. Where were her manners? Would he like a cup of tea? Did people drink tea in Sweden? Oh! What a ridiculous thing to say! Of course people drank tea in Sweden! Forgive a foolish old woman. What was wrong with her today? Pietre was ushered through the house into the kitchen where he was told to sit down and make himself at home whilst she made the tea for them all. She explained that Harold, her husband, was in the house also -she had told him about her husband hadn't she? Of course I did – silly woman! - And he was a stickler for his tea as most men were! Oh! Sorry for the assumption that all men were like her Harold!

Pietre smiled to himself as he watched Maud scuttling around the rather nice kitchen. As he waited for the tea Pietre looked around him and was pleasantly surprised by what he saw. The kitchen was, indeed, a lovely room. The rest of the house had also looked to be decorated with the same understated good taste. At least he thought it was because, in truth, Maud had hurried him into this room with almost indecent haste! Suddenly Pieter's attention was caught by the sudden appearance of a very imposing gentleman walking into the kitchen. Pietre stood up and introduced himself.

Harold Carrington shook hands with the stranger but seemed a little reticent. Harold always took his time assessing new people and this time was no exception. As an ex-military man Harold possessed an aura of authority about him that some people found unnerving. Harold was pleasantly surprised by the strength of the other man's handshake and also of the fact that the stranger in front of him held his gaze.

Harold Carrington did not have any time for people who wouldn't look him in the eye or, worse still, had a feeble handshake. He always said that you could tell the character of a man by the strength of his handshake and his ability to look you straight in the eye. In those few seconds Harold Carrington decided that he would give the stranger the benefit of the doubt. He seemed to be a decent sort of fellow. After all his beloved Maud had told him a little about the man and Harold's curiosity had got the better of him. He could have left the farmhouse once his daughter and family had left for Paris but his interest had been piqued and he had decided to check out this Swedish fellow for himself!

Pietre Mortennson was also a good judge of character, or at least he liked to think that he was, and he immediately took a liking to the stranger in front of him. Maud had explained, during one of their meetings at the local church, that both she and Harold were quite new to the area and could he see his way to ,possibly, forgiving her husband if, when they first met, he was a little stand offish? He was a good man but he didn't suffer fools gladly and she had given up trying to change him after all these years!

The mutual scrutiny was brought to an end as Maud announced that they would be having their tea in the lounge. Was that O.K. with everyone? Over the next hour or so Maud had explained that Pietre was searching for his ancestors whom, he thought, had originated from this area, and she had volunteered her services, if that was alright with Harold? Pietre then told Harold and Maud what little he already knew about his forbears and his hopes and aspirations regarding what he might discover.

As he walked slowly back to his room in the bed and breakfast Pietre kept thinking about his day. He had been most reluctant to knock on the door at first but, to his intense surprise, he had really enjoyed himself in the company of Harold and Maud Carrington and he hoped that their fledgling relationship would develop into something more substantial. The only cloud on the horizon was the strange feeling he had had when Maud had insisted on giving him the guided tour of the house and he had entered the room that Gerry, her son in law, used as a study! Oh! She was absolutely certain that Elspeth and Gerry wouldn't mind! Hadn't they told them to use the place as if it was their own whilst they were away? They were only too pleased that the house would not be left unoccupied for the next few weeks and was it O.K that their own house would be unoccupied whilst they were here? Maud had told her daughter not to worry. Harold would go along to their little cottage every day to check up on it. Anyone foolish enough to attempt a break in would endure the full wrath and fury of ex-Colonel Harold Carrington! And that fate would be infinitely worse than any custodial sentence her Majesty's government could hand out!

Pietre smiled as he remembered the look on Maud's face but his smile disappeared as he recalled his feelings on entering that room. The temperature seemed to drop. The air in the room became almost impossible to breath! He had difficulty in listening to Maud's voice! What the hell happened in that room? Pietre prided himself on his ability to rationalise things. He knew that there was always a rational explanation for everything. So what the hell was going on in that room? As he closed the door to his room Pietre Mortennson began to wonder just what lay ahead of him in his search for his ancestors.

Chapter 2.

The next morning, after a fitful night trying to surrender to sleep, Pietre and Maud set off for the library at Thetford. Pietre had made an appointment with the Senior Genealogist at the library for 10 o'clock and, as they entered the building just before 10, Pietre wondered just what he might find! The experience at "Haven's Retreat" the previous day was still playing on his mind and he did not hear Maud's voice as she asked him how he was feeling. "Sorry Maud I was miles away smiled Pietre as he looked at the concern on the old woman's face. "Are you sure you're O.K Pietre? You seem very distracted this morning! Did you sleep alright? Because if you didn't I'm absolutely certain that Gerry and Elspeth would have no objections to you staying with us in the big house whilst they are away. "I'm fine Maud; honestly. I'm just excited and not a little apprehensive about what, if anything, I might find today. That's all." Pietre flashed Maud his most disarming smile and he hoped he had convinced her. Maud Carrington looked Pietre Mortennson straight in the eye for a long few seconds and Pietre held his breath! The last thing he needed, or wanted, right now was to try to explain to anyone just exactly how he felt. He didn't know himself and so he would have found it impossible to explain anything coherently right now. Maud's face relaxed into an easy smile and she held his arm as they both went through to the library.

Oscar Washington led them through to a small ante room just off the main part of the Reference library. He was a small, wiry, man of 50 who had spent the last 25 years at Thetford library. He had started out as a newly qualified librarian here and he had, quietly and carefully, moved up the ranks until he had been made Chief Librarian in charge of Genealogy some 5 years before. Oscar had felt a great sense of personal pride that day. He was not an overly ambitious man and he knew that he would spend the rest of his career here (always allowing for Government cuts that is!).

"Mr Mortennson. How lovely to meet you in person at last. I feel as if I already know you, a little, from our past correspondences. It is so fulfilling to meet with another person who seems as interested in Genealogy as I am. Don't you think it is a most fascinating thing? Genealogy. I must admit to having more than a passing interest in your story and I have taken the liberty, if it's O.K with you, of assembling a few archive documents in readiness of your visit. Please follow me in here. I have booked the room out for the rest of the day. I wasn't quite sure how much time you would have and so I wanted to err on the side of caution. Oh! You don't have to stay all day if it's not convenient. I just wanted you to have as much time as you needed. Can I offer you and the lovely lady something to drink? Strictly against the rules you know. But who cares eh? Rules are meant to be broken as they say!"

As Oscar left to fetch drinks, that Pietre and Maud didn't really want, Pietre looked at Maud and noticed the corners of her mouth struggling to remain straight. Maud caught Pieter's eyes and suddenly they were both giggling like naughty schoolchildren.

"What a delightful little man" said Maud and then a look of horror crossed her face! "How awfully patronising did that sound? What I meant to say was that his enthusiasm was delightful to see. I don't think I have ever met a more enthusiastic Civil Servant before.

I'm certain that we have struck gold with Mr Washington. Don't you?" Before he had the chance to reply Oscar Washington came back with a tray of coffee and an unopened packet of digestive biscuits. When he saw the expression on his guest's faces Oscar Washington felt a little foolish. What had come over him? He would have had a very stern word with his staff if he had caught any of them bringing drinks into the Archive Library. Strictly forbidden. As he set the tray down in a safe corner of the room, away from any chance of spillage, Oscar Washington beckoned for his guests to take a seat at the long desk in front of them. Arranged in meticulous order lay several files, together with some computer discs, and a large notepad.

As Pietre and Maud emerged into the sunlight some 4 hours later they were both exhausted. Oscar, as he had insisted they must call him, had turned out to be an absolute godsend. He had patiently explained the system that the Library used for accessing old certificates and he had watched indulgently as both Pieter and Maud had grappled with the technology for the first hour or so. Pietre had impressed Oscar with his ability on a computer and Pietre did not have the heart to explain that the system they used in Sweden was, actually, more advanced and sophisticated than the one here in Thetford! Oscar had, rather reluctantly, left them to their own devices as he was needed in another part of the library. "The devil makes work for idle hands" was the last thing Oscar said to them both before he dashed off.

Oscar Washington had made a good impression on both of them that morning and they both, secretly, hoped that he would continue to delight them whenever they came back to Thetford.

On the journey back to Saham Toney Pietre discovered more about his new friend and her family. He learnt that they had only moved here a few months ago but, already, they felt a part of village life.

Maud told him a little about the circumstance regarding her family's reasons for going to Paris and Pietre had listened with horror as Maud had unburdened herself a little to him. He felt a great deal of affection for Maud and Harold which surprised him greatly. How could he feel such empathy for these strangers and not feel any sort of emotion for his own family back in Sweden? As Maud finished her tale she looked nervously at Pietre. What had she done? Why had she spoken as she had? What would this comparative stranger think about the ramblings of a foolish old woman? Pietre Mortennson looked Maud Carrington full in the face for several seconds before he spoke. When he spoke it was with compassion and understanding and, before he knew it, he was telling her a little about his life in Sweden and about some of the difficult times he had had recently. "What the hell was going on here? He had never spoken so truthfully and honestly before to anyone. Why was he doing this now? And with an almost total stranger!

Before long the journey back to Saham Toney was almost over and suddenly both Pietre and Maud seemed a little awkward in each other's company. The taxi driver asked where they needed to be dropped off and Maud made a split second decision. As she slid open the privacy glass, which, thankfully, had protected them from the taxi driver overhearing their conversation, Maud announced that he should stop at the bed and breakfast hotel and wait for them there whilst her friend gathered his belongings, settled his bill, and then he was to drive them on to "Haven's Retreat". "No argument young man." Said Maud with such a determined expression on her face that even if Pietre had wanted to refuse he would not have had the courage! In truth Pietre was only too delighted to spend more time with the Carrington's. The only thing that worried him was the fact that Gerry's computer was in the room that had so unsettled him the day before! What should he do about that he wondered? Don't be so foolish Pietre he said to himself. You are a rational, educated man who should know better than to worry over silly things like that.

And so it was that Mr Pietre Mortennson of Sweden became the latest guest at "Haven's Retreat".

No-one that day could have foreseen just what lay in store for them all.

Early that evening, just as the sun was leaving the sky bathed in an impressive array of pinks and oranges Pietre Mortennson laid on the bed in the guest room that Maud had simply insisted was just perfect for him and wondered what he was to do next. Around him lay the scattered remnants of his feverish meanderings through the myriad of paperwork he had amassed during his search for his ancestry. As he surveyed the detritus surrounding him he was almost overwhelmed by the task ahead. There was so much information to be dealt with that he doubted he would ever get through it all .And then he remembered the look of steely determination that had crossed the faces of both Harold and Maud. Harold had been coerced into helping them by the redoubtable Maud and, if truth be told, Harold had not put up much of a struggle. He had admitted to Pietre during a brief respite in Maud's insistence that everything would be hunky dory that he was feeling a little at a loss as to what to do with his time now that his beloved daughter and her family had gone away. He kept himself busy doing bits and pieces of nothing but he was a little bored with his lot as he had so succinctly put it. He was a military man who liked nothing better than a project to sink his teeth into!

Pietre relaxed a little as he realised that, whether he wanted it or not, Harold and Maud had decided that they would help him as much as they possibly could. As he descended the stairs to eat his supper, "Supper will be ready on the dot of 7 young Man! Don't be late." Maud had told him imperiously and so here he was with just moments to spare coming down to supper. He had dressed for the evening in his only smart clothes and he wondered if his hosts would appreciate the effort he had made. Pietre Mortennson was an extremely wealthy young man but he had little interest in fashion, clothes or indeed for the social niceties expected from him by his parents. His parents! That was a laugh! The people he had thought of as his parents had been lying to him his entire life!

Pietre made a concerted effort to shake of these negative thoughts. Tonight was not the right time to be thinking about his so called parents. But when was the right time he wondered as he opened the door to the kitchen and was assailed by the most delicious smell! Maud was bustling around the kitchen with a most determined look on her face. Harold, meanwhile, had been dispatched to the wine cellar to fetch the most suitable bottle of wine to go with the beef. As he looked on Harold reappeared with several bottles of expensive looking wine. Pietre decided not to inform his guests that he considered himself a connoisseur of fine wines.

He knew that this sounded almost pretentious but he had developed his taste for wines during his time at university.

He had had an almighty crush on Sylvia Hendrickson whom he had met when they both studied at the same university. Sylvia had seemed so self- assured that he had told her that he knew far more about wine than he actually did! Over the next few weeks he had tried, with limited success, to discover all there was to know about fine wines. About 2 weeks into their relationship Sylvia finally put him out of his misery by explaining that she always knew just how little he had known about wines but she thought it was really sweet of him to try and learn about them for her sake.

Really sweet! REALLY SWEET!

Those 2 little words developed into their first full bloodied row. No-one liked to be thought of as sweet Pietre had tried to explain. Enigmatic, intelligent, sexy – anything but sweet! As he remembered their first row Pietre also remembered how they had made it up to each other later that night! Sylvia may have looked like an angel but, by God! She was far from that! Pietre often wondered why Sylvia didn't seem to give a damn about anything or anybody. In the end it was her lack of commitment that had ended their relationship and it had hurt Pietre deeply. He had vowed that he would never expose his inner feelings like he had done with Sylvia. The hurt he felt when the relationship ended had staggered him with its intensity. He would never understand how someone could change in so short a time. He also wondered if her sudden change had had anything to do with her Father. Sylvia had finally persuaded her Father to have dinner with them both. Sylvia's Father was in the same line of business as his own Father and Pietre was more than a little worried at the prospect of meeting the all-powerful Mr Hendrickson. Pietre would never forget the haunted look on the older man's face as Pietre had stood up to shake his hand. Pietre had stood awkwardly for several seconds with his hand outstretched. The older man's eyes never left Pieter's face but he had made no attempt to shake his hand – instead he had simply turned away and left the room without uttering a single word. Sylvia had followed him out with quiet ferocity and Pietre had had little choice but to stay in the room trying hard not to listen to the raised voices coming from somewhere in the house. Eventually Sylvia had returned with the obvious signs of tears in her eyes. She had tried to explain away her Father's behaviour saying that he had had a particularly bad day at the office and he did not feel much like company tonight and would Pietre excuse his behaviour? Pietre remembered whispering some sort of platitude directed towards Sylvia as he quickly left the house. That was the last time he had seen Sylvia. She had telephoned him a few days later from Switzerland! She went on to explain that it had been decided that she would finish her education there before deciding what she wanted to do with the rest of her life. She also told him that she had decided that he no longer played a part in her life and she hoped he would eventually understand and try to forgive her!

As he sat down to a truly delicious meal Pieter was able to forget about Sylvia for the rest of the evening. Maud and Harold were both delightful company and they seemed even more enthusiastic about his lineage than he was!

Maud had them all in fits of laughter as she did a very passable impression of Oscar Washington from the library. Harold was staggered when he discovered just how far back the records went. He had had no idea that people could access so much information. He also, sheepishly, admitted to Pietre that the prospect of using a computer filled him with complete trepidation. Pietre told him that he was not to worry as he himself was an accomplished user of the infernal machines. What he did need from Harold though was his organizational skills. Surely a man with his military background could organise their agendas to ensure the smooth running of the operation? "If that wasn't too much trouble?" Harold had positively beamed at Pietre. Of course it would not be too much trouble. He would be glad of the distraction. When did he need him to start? What did he want him to do first? What time did he want him clocking on? Harold's flurry of words stopped as both Pietre and Maud stood up from the dining table and did a very over exaggerated salute! Maud's face collapsed first as she walked around the table and gave her beloved husband an affectionate dig in the ribs. ."Oh! Harold! You should see your face!"

Pietre lay awake into the early hours. He had not enjoyed himself so much in a very long time and he came to realise that he had effectively cut himself off from interaction with people since his disastrous relationship with Sylvia. Oh! He had enjoyed the company of several young ladies since then but he had not connected on an emotional level with anyone in the way that he had connected to Maud and Harold. He really enjoyed their company. He knew that, whatever else happened during his time in Norfolk, he had made some true friends here in the little village of Saham Toney.

The next morning dawned brightly and Pietre felt more relaxed than he had done in ages. The sun rising brightly seemed to set the scene for the day. Pietre was looking forward to visiting the local church and speaking to the Reverend Wellbeloved about his possible ancestors. Maud had informed him that she had taken the liberty of asking the vicar if it was possible to view the Parish records sometime in the next few days. As he descended the stairs he heard both Maud and Harold discussing him. Pietre stood just outside of the kitchen and could hardly contain his delight as he heard them saying just how nice it was to have had the opportunity to spend time with him. He was like a breath of fresh air Maud said. Harold had agreed that it was most opportune that Pietre had entered their lives just as they had time on their hands. What else were they going to do now that Elspeth and the rest of them had gone off to Paris? Pietre opened the kitchen door with a flourish and had to look down at the floor as he saw the look of horror cross the face of Maud. Oh God! Had he heard them discussing him in that way? What would he think of them? Pietre saved them both from further embarrassment by saying that he was sorry he was so late coming down for breakfast but he had slept so soundly after a wonderful time the night before. Would they both forgive him? "Nothing to forgive young man." said Harold as he ushered Pietre into a seat at the kitchen table where Maud had laid on a breakfast fit for a king! "As my dear husband would say. An Army marches on its stomach. And although I don't think we will be going into battle with the Reverend Wellbeloved it doesn't do any harm to have a full tummy. Does it?"

As Pietre tucked heartily into his breakfast little did any of them know just what lay ahead for them all!

Chapter 3.

The Reverend Wellbeloved took his time dressing that morning. He wondered why he was taking particular care that morning and then he remembered why. Maud Carrington had been a member of his congregation for a comparatively short time but she had certainly made her mark! She had telephoned him the previous day to inform him that she would be arriving with her new friend from Sweden that morning. The Reverend Wellbeloved had been left in no doubt that Maud Carrington expected him to be ready for their visitor. As he re-knotted his tie for the third time the Reverend Wellbeloved smiled to himself. He had not realised the complexities involved in trying to run a provincial parish such as this. Oh! The politics involved startled him. Would he ever master the subtle nuances involved in trying to appease everybody? He wondered if he would ever get it right. He knew that he was well prepared for the morning ahead. He prided himself on his organisational skills. He had contacted the Bishop prior to today and had the authorisation to release some of the Parish records regarding the lineage of Pietre Mortennson. The Bishop had received a communication from a colleague in Stockholm requesting his co-operation. It seemed that the redoubtable Pietre Mortennson had donated a not inconsiderable sum of money towards the restoration fund for his local church on the understanding that he would expect the very best co-operation from the church in this matter. The Reverend Wellbeloved checked his appearance in the mirror one last time and came to the conclusion that he did, indeed, look as though he knew what he was doing. Appearances could be deceptive he mused as he put on his coat and headed towards the church.

Maud Carrington felt the same level of spirituality she always felt when entering the church. She had always enjoyed her faith but had come to realise that her faith meant more to her with the passing of the years. She looked at Pietre as he walked towards the altar. She wondered just how much faith meant to him. Was he only concerned with finding out about his background? Or was his interest more than that? She hoped that it was. As the Reverend Wellbeloved shook hands with Pietre the emotions going on between them all could not have been more different and varied. Maud hoped that Pietre would "find" religion. The Reverend Wellbeloved hoped that, somehow, he would be instrumental in helping Pietre Morgennson find his long lost relatives. Pietre, meanwhile, hoped that today would not be a complete waste of time! He had come a long way in his research for his long lost relatives and he hoped that today would be more fruitful than he had the right to expect.

All of their hopes would be answered in more ways than they could ever have imagined!

As the morning progressed it became evident that Pieter's family had an inexplicable history with Saham Toney. He discovered that his great-great-great grandparents had been born here and had, in fact, been married from the very same church he now stood in! Pietre could not comprehend what was in front of his eyes. The marriage certificate he was looking at confirmed that he was a direct descendant of the people of Saham Toney! His ancestors Joshua and Flora had been married in the exact same spot that he stood in!

Joshua Bromfield had married Flora Gibson in this church! Pietre looked around him and tried to imagine how his great-great-great grandparents must have felt as they walked down the aisle to start married life together? He wondered just what they were like. What did they do in the village? Did they both work for a living? All these thoughts and many more crowded into Pieter's mind as he walked around the church. He had begun to wonder about his real parents. Since his parents had died he had wondered just who he was. Maybe being here would help him to find his roots. Pieter decided at that very moment that he would use every means available to get to the bottom of who he was. He was luckier than many because of his wealth. He had never really appreciated it before but now he realised the potential of his cash. He would have the very real chance of discovering all about his family. Maud interrupted his thoughts by asking him if he was feeling O.K. Pieter's mind slowly came back to the present time. He had realised that he had walked out of the church without a word to either Maud or the vicar. Now he found himself standing in the centre of the churchyard trying to find the gravestone of either Joshua or Flora. The graveyard was not a particularly big one and it did not take him long to realise that any headstone that may have been there was no longer! Adrian Wellbeloved had followed closely by Pieter as he had looked in vain. He had not discovered a gravestone for either of them. His research had ended there but he realised the importance of finding out further information and so he was able to tell Pieter that he had access to further records that were held in Thetford. An appointment had been arranged again at Thetford for 2 days' time.

Maud declared that that was a splendid idea. Today would be the day to fill in as many gaps as possible using the Parish Registers. Harold would be dispatched to the supermarket for something for lunch as she had decided that as today was such a glorious day they would spend the time here in church looking over the documents. If that was alright with you vicar of course? Adrian knew when to admit defeat and, besides, the whole process intrigued him. He was able to trace his own history back centuries as none of his forebears seemed to have any foresight regarding the outside world. His great-great grandparents must have caused a minor scandal when they moved 20 miles away from the village to set up home together after their marriage. Adrian had also discovered that by the time the next census came around his ancestors were to be found living back in his sleepy village in Somerset!

As the evening shadows cast their long shadows over the vicarage garden Pieter decided that enough was enough for today. He had made some progress, more than he could have hoped for, but he had hit a complete brick wall trying to find out about his Father's side. He had always been told that his parent's families had all come from England generations ago. So why could he not find anything out about his Father's side. Pietre decided that he would telephone Sweden and employ someone from the Agency he had used to obtain the information he now had and he would get them to delve deeper. Somewhere there should be records regarding the sea voyage from Norfolk. There should be some evidence of exactly when his forebears had come to Sweden. He would pay handsomely for this information, but, he knew –somehow– that he needed it quickly.

The next morning, after a productive telephone call to Sweden, Pietre called in at the vicarage to say thank you for the previous day. As he walked towards the vicarage Pietre took a detour through the graveyard.

The sun was casting shadows around the graveyard as Pietre walked slowly through the oldest part of the graveyard. He looked, dispassionately, at the headstones and then he gasped! He knelt down to check that what he thought he had read was correct. There in front of him was a headstone that told of the death of a woman who shared the same surname as one of his ancestors. Who was she? Was she any relation? How could he possibly find out? How had he missed it yesterday?

Pietre sat quietly at the desk in the church and watched as the Reverend Wellbeloved carefully opened the old Parish Register. The permission for which had been granted that very morning. It was amazing what the mention of a very generous donation could achieve thought Pietre wryly. Oh! Well! What was money for? If not for easing you through your day, mused Pietre?

Adrian Wellbeloved had been both surprised, and delighted, to hear about Pieter's generous donation. He had been even more surprised to discover that there were records regarding the old graveyard still here in the Church. He was glad that his own curiosity had got the better of him and he had gone in search of more evidence in the Church's archives. The old cupboard where he had found out the information had not been opened in years judging by the musty smell that assailed his nostrils when he had first opened the door. As he was quite new to the Parish he had been completely unaware of the cupboards existence. His predecessor had been suffering from memory loss and the onset of dementia for years before the Church made the decision to release him from his duties. The members of the congregation who helped out had not thought to tell him of the cupboard and its contents as, quite reasonably; they assumed that the records held little or no significance to most people here in Saham Toney. After all most of the residents had lived here all their lives. They knew who was buried here and where to find them after all!

The Reverend Wellbeloved reluctantly left Pietre to his research. He was intrigued by what Pietre might find. He hoped that his help would be useful. As he looked back Pieter's face was a picture of concentration. He had not even noticed the vicar's departure.

Pietre looked at the document in front of him. A copy of the marriage certificate of his great-great grandparents. As he stared at it Pieter's mind began to wonder just what life had been like for them both.

July 1st 1806.

Flora woke that morning with the same sense of wonder she had felt since that fateful day some 12 months before when Joshua Bromfield had asked her Father for her hand in marriage! She had held her breath waiting for her Father's answer. She respected her Father very much but she also knew that, if he had refused the request, he was not a man to change his mind! Her Mother had taken it upon herself to arrange everything for the wedding down to the last detail and it was only because Flora adored her Mother that she allowed her Mother's indulgences. They had lived here in the village of Saham Toney all their lives and she hoped that, once she was married, they would live here for the rest of their days. As she carefully dressed that morning Flora wondered just how her life might change once she was married. Joshua Bromfield was a young and devilishly handsome farmer who could have had the pick of the entire village as well as the pick of the entire neighbourhood Flora didn't doubt. He had chosen her to be his bride! Her! Flora Gibson could not believe her luck, even now, on this her wedding morning. Nothing was going to spoil this day. Nothing!

An hour later and a truly radiant Flora became Mrs Bromfield in a simple ceremony. The reception, in contrast, was anything but simple! How her Mother had persuaded her Father to spend so much money she would never know. The table groaned under the weight of food and drink. All of her neighbours had attended and the weather had been glorious. The only thing that had troubled Flora was the chance meeting she had had with Lizzie Stump.

Lizzie had frightened Flora ever since she could remember. She seemed to have the knack of looking into Flora's soul and reading her innermost thoughts. On many occasions Lizzie had known something about Flora or her family that she couldn't possibly have known or guessed about. Lizzie was tolerated in the village by most people but not the clergy! It was rumoured that Lizzie was a witch and if she was not careful she would fall foul of the Church and she would be burnt at the stake or, at the very least, be driven out of the village.

Flora had been appalled when she had heard the local clergyman, whom she privately disliked on first sight, telling his congregation, in a thinly disguised attack on Lizzie, that only people who believed in the one true faith would enter the kingdom of heaven and all others would be damned for all eternity in the fires of hell!

Nevertheless, Flora had been startled when Lizzie had seemed to appear out of nowhere and warned her about her forthcoming nuptials. Lizzie had told her that she would never be happy living in the new house that she would one day move into. She would give birth to healthy children but tragedy would strike and she would have no option but to flee the country in fear and disgrace! Flora had listened to Lizzie's tirade in anguished silence. It was her wedding morning! She was to be the new Mrs Bromfield in less than 6 hours! What was Lizzie doing? She looked wild eyed and kept trying to pull Flora away from the house. She kept muttering about the truth will out. She would not be responsible for the tragedy that lay ahead for hadn't she, Lizzie, tried her best to talk sense into her? Hadn't' she?

That night, after the final guest had departed, Flora and Joshua shared the marital bed for the first time. Flora, being a farmer's daughter was not so naïve about the act of mating with animals but she was totally unprepared for her first night as a married woman!

Joshua Bromfield might have been dashingly handsome but he was also the least arrogant man. He had soon realised the power of a well- placed smile and that knowledge had stood him in good stead on more than one occasion! As he climbed the stairs that night it would have been impossible to guess who was the more nervous of the two! He had had the embarrassing talk with his own Father and had endured the ribald comments of his unmarried friends but he was terrified!

The next morning the newlyweds began their married life together in total harmony. The previous evening had been beautiful. Joshua had confessed his terror to his wife because, as he told her later, the sight of her tortured face gave him a fit of the giggles! Flora had laughed as she told Joshua that that was exactly what she was thinking as she saw her Husband approach the marital bed!

Joshua and Flora Bromfield started working on their smallholding that same morning. They could not afford to take time off from their work because, as Joshua told her many times, this smallholding was only the beginning because he would do everything he possible could to give the most beautiful woman in the universe everything she desired!

They were going places and the sky was the limit – just you wait and see! Flora smiled indulgently at her new Husband as he went out to tend the field.

As she stood at the kitchen window waiting for the kettle to boil so that she might clean her new dishes Flora caught sight of Lizzie Stump staring straight at her from the trees at the far end of their land. Lizzie just stared and stared and Flora was reminded of the other woman's proclamation. Don't be so stupid thought Flora as she busied herself about the house. Everyone knew that Lizzie was a bit strange and most folks took precious little notice of her- so why did she feel so unsettled? Why was the sight of mad Lizzie Stump upsetting her so? Flora wrapped her shawl tightly around her shoulders and went out to join her Husband on the first day of their new life together. Nothing would spoil today or the rest of their lives together – especially Lizzie Stump!

Chapter 4.

August 2012.

When the Reverend Wellbeloved came back into the church some 4 hours later he was more than a little startled to see that Pietre was still engrossed in the Church archives! "My goodness me! Are you still here Pietre? I thought you would have left ages ago! Oh! I don't mean that you need to go now. It's just that I didn't think there would be enough information here for you to get much further with your research. You look as though you've found something. May I?" The Reverend Wellbeloved sat himself down besides Pietre and he had the most expectant look on his face that Pietre didn't have the heart to disappoint him. Pietre had hoped to tell Harold and Maud about his possible discovery but he realised that the Reverend Wellbeloved was not going anywhere for the time being!

When he eventually got back to "Haven's Retreat" Pietre could not help but wonder about the place. The building was exactly the right age (as were many more buildings in the village thought Pietre to himself) the "feel" of the building was what bothered Pietre the most. Maud came into the lounge with a tray of steaming coffee and some delightful homemade biscuits. The meal that they had just had had been excellent and generous and Pietre wondered if he would have any room for coffee let alone biscuits! Maud had told him that she was dying to know how he had got on at the Church but she was busy with the dishes and they would chat later! As he sat down in the armchair nearest the French windows Pietre looked out at the beautiful garden. Whenever he walked in it the garden seemed to ease his mind. He had never really appreciated the beauty and tranquillity of a garden before now but he knew that, when he got back to Sweden (if he got back there!) WHERE HAD THAT COME FROM? Then he would make certain that he bought a house with a garden.

His thoughts were interrupted by a discreet cough coming from the direction of Harold and Maud who had appeared at his side without him realising it! He really must concentrate more! What was wrong with him? He was not usually like this – but then he was not normally to be found in Norfolk researching people who may, or may not, be related to him.

Maud was fascinated by what Pietre told them. She was convinced that there must be some sort of connection between Pieter's ancestors and this house." How exciting my dear! Aren't you excited Harold? Oh! Of course you aren't. Why should you be? You old stick in the mud! Well I'm excited enough for all three of us! Please tell me there is something I can do to help! I know I'm an interfering old busybody but I can't help but feel that you are onto something here and I just want to help in whatever small way that I can. You don't mind do you? Oh! Please say that you don't mind my helping"

The look of delighted expectation written all over Maud's face made Pietre laugh out loud. When he saw the look of consternation and embarrassment cross over Maud's face he was at pains to tell her that of course she could help. He would only be too grateful for whatever help she might like to give. And so it was settled that the very next morning Mrs Maud Carrington was to be put in charge of visiting the library at Thetford once more and her task was to unearth as much information regarding "Haven's Retreat" as was humanly possible.

As Harold said his goodnight to Pietre he gave the younger man a look that seemed to suggest that he didn't realise just what he had let himself in for! Harold knew his wife very well and he had recognised that look of steely determination before. Woe betides anyone who tried to stop Mrs Maud Carrington when she was on a mission. As he climbed the stairs Harold was more than a little envious of them both. Don't be such an old fool thought Harold. They don't want an old codger like me getting in the way. Do they? But hadn't he got the organisational skills needed for a job such as this? Hadn't he got as much time on his hands as his beloved wife and weren't two minds better than one in a case like this?

As he undressed Harold decided that he had never shied away from a battle before and he wasn't about to start now! He would offer his services the next day and, By Jove, he wasn't taking no for an answer!

September 1st 1807.

Flora Bromfield inched her way slowly out of bed. She tried not to disturb her beloved Joshua who slept peacefully at her side. She needed to pass water! She needed to pass water very urgently. As she made her way outside to the evil smelling part of the house she gave way to the grin that had been trying its best to escape from her mouth. She was pregnant! SHE WAS WITH CHILD! Flora had begun to wonder if it would ever happen. She had been married for a while before becoming pregnant and the gossip had already started! Was she barren? Would Joshua leave her for someone who could give him an heir? When she had mentioned her concerns to Joshua she had been astounded by his reaction. He had shouted and yelled at her for the first and, as yet, only time in their brief marriage. Why did people think it was their business discussing their marriage? Who do they think they are? They had only been married for a short while hadn't they?

Flora had been both shocked and frightened by the vehemence of her Husband's reaction and she had steered clear of mentioning it again. Joshua had, eventually, calmed down and all seemed to be getting back to normal until the other night. In her dreams Flora had encountered Lizzie Stump - the woman who had tried to warn her of some terrible fate just before her wedding day. In her nightmare Lizzie kept repeating over and over again like some terrible mantra that no good would come of her marriage and no joy would come from her pregnancy! Flora had awoken from this traumatic night with a deep sense of foreboding that she had not been able to shake off all day. When she had eventually fallen asleep after a long and tiring day Flora had fallen almost instantly into a dreamless sleep. She had been so sound asleep that when she eventually disturbed she knew that she was desperately in urgent need of passing water!

As she climbed the stairs on her way back to bed Flora thought back to her wedding day. Why had she dreamt about Lizzie after all this time? Why now when she should have been so happy?

Joshua watched his wife as she left the bedroom through half closed eyes. He had feigned sleep. Why? Joshua knew why. He was a worried man. A very worried man! He should have told Flora when they were first married. He should have been honest with her from the beginning and now it was too late. His wife was having a baby! What was he thinking of? What if the gift (or the curse more like!) was transferred to the baby? What would he do then? He had spent all his life running away from his gift and he did not know what to do. How he wished he was more like Lizzie Stump.

Joshua Bromfield had the gift of second sight – he also had the power to hear the dead!

He had hated his gift all his life but he acknowledged that he was powerless to stop the voices in his head or the images in his brain. He blocked them out as often as he could but the images he had had recently seen were too horrific to ignore! His own child – born with such disfigurement that everyone would see that the child (Joshua knew with absolute certainty that his unborn child was a girl!) was a witch! Everyone knew that a child with six fingers on each hand was a witch. Everyone KNEW that – didn't they? Joshua wondered what to do. He had to do something to protect both himself and his precious family. But how? How could he make this right? As he heard Flora coming up the stairs Joshua turned away from the door and feigned sleep again. He must make a decision. He must make a decision soon. Joshua knew that the destiny of his family lay in his hands and he was afraid!

After an early breakfast that day Joshua drove the horse and carriage the 20 miles to the nearest hamlet where his beloved Parent's still lived. As he came to the small cottage that had been his home until he had married some 6 months earlier Joshua stopped and drew breath. He had never discussed his "gift" with his Parent's before. Oh! He suspected that they would not be surprised, only disappointed and worried, that the ability to see and hear the dead had been passed on to the next generation.

Alfred and Jessica – Joshua's parents - had only been "courting" a short while when the spectre of the "gift" reared its head. Jessica had been appalled and terrified when the vision of her Fiancée's newly deceased Grandmother had appeared to her in the kitchen of Alfred's home. The old lady kept repeating that they must not get married! They cannot get married! Only pain and misery would happen if they were allowed to be wed. Jessica had never spoken to another soul about her talent – if that is what it could be called- and she was astounded when a few moments later she heard Alfred telling his deceased Grandmother to please keep quiet because he needed time to think! Jessica had hidden just outside the kitchen and had been further astonished when she heard Alfred talking to his Grandmother who had passed away the previous summer and she heard his Grandmother's reply! Jessica was so shocked at this that she let out a strangled cry and Alfred realised that she must have heard him talking to himself. Imagine his shock when Jessica had finally admitted that not only could she hear his late Grandmother but she could see her too! Alfred had nearly fallen off his chair at that. He admitted that he could hear her but he could not see her. After the initial shock Alfred and Jessica both agreed to keep their little secret safe. Alfred was particularly concerned for Jessica's safety as he was convinced that, if anyone in the village were to find out, then his beloved would be burnt at the stake as a witch!

Alfred was only too aware of the double standards involved as he was also absolutely certain that no-one would suspect him, a man, of having similar "skills". A few years later Joshua had been born and both his Parent's silently prayed that their child would be spared. Alas it was not to be. Joshua quickly showed signs of being even more adept than either of his Parent's. From a very early age Joshua would strike up random conversations with different people. At first his Parent's had been able to disguise this as a small child who had an overactive imagination but, as Joshua grew, this became impossible to continue as Joshua would insist that he could hear people talking to him and asking questions all the time! After some terrible soul searching it was decided that they must leave immediately. Alfred was absolutely convinced that people were talking about them and he was certain that if anyone saw for themselves the animated conversations that their beloved Joseph had with his "imaginary" friends then people would be convinced that they had a possessed family in their midst. As it turned out Alfred's suspicions were correct and that fateful day would stay in the memory of all of them until their dying day. The village had turned against them. Every last man, woman and child had turned into a baying mob. Alfred had grabbed his wife and child and dashed to his horse and cart and fled as quickly as the old horse could take them. Alfred could still hear the threats loud in his ear. How could people be so cruel? Threatening to kill all of them! What had happened to his neighbours who had appeared to be kind, gentle people? How could they change into this rabid mob?

After that fateful night Joshua had never spoken about his gift again. He made a conscious decision to never let his Parent's see him in "conversation" with his ghosts, or whatever you needed to label them, and over the years he had been convinced that, whilst his Parent's may still have a slight suspicion, neither his beloved Mother and Father knew for certain just how adept he had become in hiding the true level of his ability.

Joshua squared his shoulders and knocked gently on the door.

Flora wondered just where her Husband had got too. He had been gone all day. She knew that he had mentioned going over to see his Mother and Father soon but she had assumed, not unreasonably, that they would both go together before she became too immobile to travel. Flora wanted her first child to be born in their little cottage and had told Joshua that she would not venture far until the baby was born. As the light began to fade the first trickle of doubt and concern edged its way slowly down her spine. Don't be so fanciful she scolded herself. She was being silly. This baby was making her mind do funny things. Flora got herself ready for bed but knew that sleep would escape her. She had not been alone out here before and she could not shake of this feeling of foreboding that was beginning to envelop her and threatened to overwhelm her at any minute. Where was Joshua? He should have been home by now. Night had settled in and she could not see a thing from out of her bedroom window. As she lay in bed looking through the window Flora eventually drifted into a fitful sleep that was filled with startling images of her baby being born and taken from her by force. She was powerless to stop whoever it was from getting away with her little girl! How was she so certain that it was a girl? Where was Joshua? This niggling pain was getting more intense by the minute. She knew that she should try to get help but she had no idea where to go. The cottage was isolated; she was alone and in pain. What was she going to do?

Flora had not realised that she had cried out in agony. She had not realised that people were in her bedroom looking concerned. She was delirious with pain. Where was Joshua? Why was he not here with her? Who was tending to her? As she slowly focussed her eyes Flora silently screamed and something inside her froze! Lizzie Stump was leaning over her and the look on her face was one that Flora would never forget. Lizzie was chanting and wailing as she began to prepare Flora for the imminent arrival of her first born child. Flora vaguely recognised the other women in the room. They were all related to Lizzie and they were all chanting and wailing in the same terrible way. Flora closed her eyes and tried to block out the images with little success. Why was she in so much pain? She knew that childbirth was both painful and dangerous but, surely, this level of pain was unbearable.

Several hours later Flora woke from a fitful sleep to discover that the room was quiet and everyone except Lizzie had left. Lizzie Stump was bustling about and was unaware that Flora had woken. Flora lay quietly as she tried to gather her thoughts. The pain had subsided somewhat and this thought should have comforted her but it made Flora feel terrified. She had given birth-that much she was certain of- so where was her baby and why was Lizzie Stump here?

Almost as if she had read her thoughts Lizzie replied that yes she had given birth to a beautiful, healthy little girl some 3 hours ago and the little one was being cared for by Lizzie's Mother and Auntie downstairs. At this Flora tried to get out of bed but Lizzie was too quick for her. Within seconds Lizzie's face appeared inches from her face and the quiet venom in her voice chilled Flora's blood. "Didn't I tell you? What did I say? Nothing good would come of you having a child! I have known all along about your "special gift" my dear. And of your Husband's "special gift". For don't I possess the same affliction myself my dear?" The look of triumph on the other woman's face did nothing to quell the awful dread in the pit of Flora's stomach. "What do you mean? I don't know what you are talking about. What sort of special gift? Where's my child? What have you done with her? Where's Joshua? What have you done with them both?" The blow to her face stunned her into silence. Lizzie had hit her – hard. "Let me tell you something dearie. Your little secret is safe with me, for the time being, on one condition. That little innocent girl lying downstairs will go from here tonight and you will never see her again. She must surely have exceptional powers and she will be very useful to all of the others here in the village who share our gift. Oh! Don't look so shocked. People think that I am simple and stupid and should be ignored or tolerated but my dearie I am neither simple nor stupid. It suits our purpose to let the ignorant peasants in the village think that they have the upper hand but, believe me, they have no idea just what the birth of this child will do for our coven. Oh Yes! You needn't look so surprised. I am a witch. You are a witch with; possibly, greater powers than I possess. Your first born child will have exceptional powers! Even greater powers than either of us can imagine! She will be taken away from here and you will tell your Husband that the child was stillborn and that I helped you when I heard your cry for help! Do I make myself clear? Well do I?"

Flora wondered just how she had survived the night as she struggled to remember the events of the previous evening. She remembered that Lizzie had forced her to drink some foul potion that seemed to drain every ounce of strength from her so she could only watch help helplessly as Lizzie and her family cleaned every trace of themselves from her house. Flora's last, vague, memory was of Lizzie coming once more to her bedside and reminding her of what she would do to her and her Husband if they ever mentioned the events of tonight to anyone!

Joshua woke early the next morning and knew, instinctively, that he must head for home. Now! He made his excuses to his Parents, studiously avoiding any eye contact, and began his long journey home.

As dusk settled on the horizon Joshua breathed a sigh of relief. The cottage was in sight. He was home at last. So why did this feeling of dread still hang around him? He should be happy that he was home at last. He should be thankful to be in the loving embrace of his beloved wife. Why did it take all his strength to open the front door? As he called Flora's name he realised that something was wrong. Something was terribly wrong! As he slowly climbed the stairs he began to hear a sound. At first he did not recognise it as human but as he slowly pushed open the door to their bedroom Joshua was appalled to see the prostrate body of his wife weeping and wailing on the bedroom floor.

A little over an hour later and Joshua was sitting on the floor staring into space. He could not believe what he had heard. He would NOT believe what he had heard! Lizzie Stump had taken his child away. Lizzie Stump had admitted to being a witch and she knew about their "special" gift. What was he to do? What could he do? He had finally persuaded Flora to climb into bed where he had held her tightly until she had surrendered to sleep. As he looked at Flora's sleeping form he knew what he had to do. He knew that NOBODY was going to take his child away. Whatever it took Joshua knew that their child would be found and returned to them. The look of grim determination on Joshua's face echoed the call of his heart. He had this evil gift and his beautiful wife had this evil gift. He knew, without a doubt, that their beautiful, innocent daughter must possess the gift. That is why she had been taken. That was why he needed to save her from the clutches of Lizzie stump and her odious family.

As the first rays of sun bathed the bedroom in warm, golden shadows the temperature in Joshua's heart could not have contrasted more. He had made a plan. It would involve danger. It would mean that they must leave the village forever and start a new life once again! But it would be worth it – wouldn't it? After checking that Flora was comfortable and not in danger of her life Joshua made Flora promise that she would lock herself in the house and under no circumstances was she to let anyone over the threshold. She should pack as few possessions as she could and she should be ready to leave at a moment's notice. Flora had cried and begged and pleaded with him but to no avail. His mind was made up.

He would be back just before nightfall if he was lucky and she should be ready to leave immediately. As he remembered the anguished look on his dear wife's face Joshua hoped with all his heart that he would have the courage to do what he knew he must. With a heavy heart and a backward glance he set of to find Lizzie Stump!

Chapter 5.

September 2012.

Pietre lay awake in the guest bedroom of Haven's Retreat and looked at the ceiling. He wondered just how many other people over the centuries had done the exact same thing. He wondered how many of them had been as troubled as he was. Absent mindedly he began to rub together the scars he had on both hands. He had often asked his parents, or rather the people who had pretended to be his parents; about the symmetrical scars he had just to the side of his little fingers. What had happened to him? Why did he have scars? His parents had evaded and avoided the questions until he had simply given up asking any more.

Pietre knew that he was being unreasonable and perhaps a little foolish but he had begun to wonder if this house had something to do with his scars itching as they did. He had realised, with a jolt, that EVERY time he came into this house his scars became more uncomfortable. Normally he never even noticed them but recently he had begun to realise that this house had this strange effect on him. Don't be so bloody ridiculous he chastised himself as he hauled himself out of the ridiculously comfy bed he had slept in. This house had nothing to do with his scars. He vowed to tell no-one about his fanciful thoughts. He knew how ridiculous they sounded in his own head. How crazy would they sound if he said them out loud? As the smell of a full English breakfast assaulted his senses Pietre headed for the shower and prepared for another day researching for his erstwhile family.

Maud and Harold had woken early that morning both with a renewed sense of energy and purpose. Maud had admitted to herself that she had a TINY crush on the enigmatic Pietre Morgennson but as she was old enough to be his Mother (no Maude – be honest – his Grandmother) she should stop all this silly nonsense and concentrate on the task at hand!

Harold, meanwhile, was looking forward to travelling with Pietre and Maud into Thetford and delving further into Pieter's family tree. Harold had never really understood anyone's fascination with discovering their long lost relations. Harold appreciated the irony of these thoughts because, being of the "old school" he could trace his lineage back centuries just by visiting the local church where he had spent his entire life before joining the Army. His ancestors had lived in the same village for hundreds of years and he was probably related to the majority of the village folk. Harold often wondered just how closely he was related to some of the people in the village because, like many well to do families, his was not without its fair share of scandal and intrigue!

Pietre came into the beautiful old kitchen and allowed the warmth of the room, and its occupants, to wash over him as he devoured yet another scrumptious breakfast laid before him. As Harold was always saying An Army cannot march into battle on an empty stomach young man!

Quite what battles Harold thought they would be up against Pietre never did ask but the sight of the two people in front of him, people he had only known for a short while but had begun to have great affection for, looking expectantly at him made him buckle down and get himself battle ready.

Oscar Washington was at his desk bright and early that morning. He was always a stickler for time but this morning he was particularly early and he was not a little unexcited himself! What was he thinking? These lovely people would not want him hovering around. He had some work to do and they had papers to look at. Oscar would never admit it to a living soul but he too had become more than a little obsessed with the divine Pietre and the sweet Harold and Maud. He had taken it upon himself to do a little research of his own. Oh! He knew that he was overstepping the mark but, What the Hell! Rules were meant to be broken surely? Oscar Washington looked around his office in case he had said these blasphemous thoughts out loud. What would his staff think if they could hear his thoughts? Rules were meant to be broken? I ask you – what is the world coming to? Despite this Oscar did allow himself a slightly indulgent smile to himself as he recalled his research. He just hoped that Pietre, Maud and Harold would appreciate his efforts but not feel obliged to thank his Superiors for the sterling work he had done without them even asking?

Thetford could never be described as inspirational to many of its visitors or residents but that day proved the critics wrong. Oscar Washington basked in the praise handed out to him by Pietre, Maud and Harold that day.

Oscar had managed to locate a birth certificate of sorts for one of Pieter's long lost relatives. This great news had been tempered with a death certificate dated three days later! It would appear that a child had been born to Joshua and Flora Bromfield in 1807. The little girl had been named Jessica. Three days later, however, a death certificate had been issued for Jessica. Oscar had explained that this was not an uncommon thing. Many children died soon after birth and Oscar had pointed out that the mother had not died in childbirth so that was surely something positive? Unfortunately his research had drawn a blank regarding the whereabouts of Joshua and Flora following this. Don't worry, I can still do some extra research and find out if they moved away if you want me to? Oscar had asked nervously. The others had thanked him profusely and agreed to meet up the following week to see what else the redoubtable Oscar had for them! Oscar Washington had felt foolishly pleased and proud to be part of the journey that these delightful people were on. He just hoped that he wouldn't get into too much trouble on the way!

September 1807.

Joshua Bromfield wrestled with his conscience. What he was about to do went against everything he held dear. He was about to commit a heinous crime and he was more than a little scared. Flora had finally succumbed to reason and drank some of the special herbal tea that he himself had prepared for her. She had screamed out loud when he had first suggested it and it had taken all of Joshua's patience and understanding to fully realise just how frightened Flora was. The last time someone had given her something herbal to drink she had slipped into unconsciousness and her baby had been taken from her! Joshua knew that the calming effects of the tea would affect his beloved wife for at least the next few hours – allowing her to organise their few belongings ready to flee at a moment's notice - by which time he hoped to be back at home- then the reality of what must be done would hit them both. It was still dark but the moonlight helped to show him the way. He was grateful for the light but the shadows cast as he walked did little to calm his already fragile nerves. He knew where he was heading to and he also knew that he must not waver in his mission. He would bring his baby back to their little cottage if it was the last thing he ever did. As this thought passed unwanted, and unneeded, through his mind Joshua's resolve hardened and he strode more purposefully towards Lizzie Stump's hovel. When he drew nearer Joshua instinctively moved more stealthily. He did not expect to just simply walk into Lizzie's home and ask her nicely for the safe return of his first born. Joshua knew just exactly what Lizzie was. He knew exactly what all her family were. What he was hoping that Lizzie did not realise, however, was the true extent of his own powers. He hated his powers with a terrible vengeance but even he could acknowledge that his way was the only way to bring his daughter back.

As he came in sight of the hovel that Lizzie called home -he slowly and deliberately withdrew the knife and the pistol he had brought with him and carefully opened the door.

Lizzie Stump was standing in the centre of the room, with an older woman whom Joshua recognised as a relation of Lizzie's, lit only by a tiny scrap of candle that flickered alarmingly and threatened to plunge the room into inky blackness at any second. In an instant Joshua knew just what Lizzie was holding in her arms! Joshua and Lizzie stared in total silence at each other for a long moment before Joshua finally found his voice. "Lizzie Stump I think you know why I'm here." Joshua was surprised at just how calm he sounded – inside he thought he was going to pass out his body was shaking so much and his mind was whirling – but he knew that he would have only one chance to do what he came to do. "Joshua Bromfield, – only Lizzie could make the sound of his own name seem so small and helpless- I was wondering when you would call. Oh! Don't look so surprised. You forget that I know all about you and your "special gift". Did you honestly think that I would be surprised? Lizzie's laugh cut through the dank atmosphere of the dreadful place she called home and the baby began to whimper. As Lizzie looked down at the infant with malevolent eyes she took a step towards Joshua! "Would you like to look at the face of your first born for the first and only time? Let me assure you that you will not succeed in your mission to bring your baby home."

Lizzie then began to make a sound that seemed to be laughter but in fact was a primeval sound that chilled Joshua's blood in his veins. Before he knew what he was doing Joshua lunged at Lizzie. The look of surprise on her face was quickly taken over by a look of pure hatred as Lizzie deftly moved towards the embers of the fire that flickered ominously. "One more step towards me and you will regret it for the rest of your miserable life." Joshua stopped dead in his tracks. What the hell was he supposed to do now? This was not how it was meant to be! This was going horribly wrong. Lizzie Stump stood by the open fire and slowly removed the swaddling clothes that protected his baby daughter form the elements. As she continued to remove all the clothing Lizzie's eyes never once left Joshua's face. His child was only a few feet away from him but Joshua felt impotent. What could he do? As these thoughts raced around his head a new sound filled the room. Lizzie aged Aunt began wailing and moaning and Lizzie's eyes left Joshua's face for a second. In the split second that Lizzie's attention was diverted Joshua sprang into action. In one swift movement he had pinned Lizzie against the fire wall. Before he knew what was happening he had plunged the blade of his knife into her neck and was twisting and twisting with all his strength. The awful sound that emanated from her was a dreadful mixture of agony and undisguised fury. Lizzie let out a howl of utter hatred and pulled herself away from Joshua. He picked up a bowl from the kitchen table and swung it with all of his might and hit Lizzie full in the face. The bowl splintered into pieces and one of the shards was sticking out of Lizzie's cheek at an obscene angle. Lizzie seemed to barely notice - such was her rage. Joshua grabbed hold of his beloved daughter just as Lizzie began to sink slowly to her knees. Lizzie was bleeding profusely from her gaping wound but Joshua felt no pity or shame about what he had done. Instead he felt a deepening fury of his own. He would not let this creature (He would not let himself think that she was human) take his child. He would rather die here in this hovel than let that happen.

As Lizzie's aunt tended to her shrieking niece Joshua made his way to the door. Lizzie's aunt looked up at him and slowly and deliberately began a low moaning chant that became louder and higher pitched with ever second. Joshua's head felt that it would explode, such was the intensity of the sound, but then the sound stopped only to be replaced with an even more frightening sound! The sound of a gunshot!

As Joshua struggled with his baby daughter on the way home he had to sit for a while because his legs suddenly began to give way and he was violently sick. How could he have done such a terrible thing? As he lay panting for breath his thoughts turned back to a few moments ago. Lizzie's Aunt had screamed at him and hurtled towards him with a venomous look in her eyes. The sound in the tiny room had been ear shattering and his beloved daughter had begun to scream uncontrollably. The look of stunned surprise on the face of the older woman looked almost comical as she lay dead at his feet with a gaping hole in her chest that was spurting blood all over the floor. As Joshua looked at the smoke coming from his pistol he could not believe he had shot her!

Lizzie Stump had stood stock still for a few vital seconds before she had staggered towards him with the most evil, demonic, look on her face. The second shot sounded even louder than the first in the tiny room. Joshua would never forget the sight of Lizzie's face as she struggled to stand.

She was screaming incoherently in a strange tongue all the while she was trying to get to him. Joshua would never fully understand how he was capable of doing what he did next but he lashed out at Lizzie's prone body with his heavy boot and he kicked her full in the face. The sound of bone smashing and the gurgling of Lizzie's blood in her throat only served to ensure that Joshua finished what he had started. He kicked and kicked until Lizzie stopped moving.

What was that chant thought Joshua? He had not been able to decipher a single word but, somehow, he knew that the chant was something evil and malevolent and it had obviously been directed at both himself and his precious daughter.

Joshua knew that both women must be dead! How could anyone survive such terrible injuries? Surely even a witch as powerful as Lizzie could not live after what he had done to her?

All Joshua knew was that he, Flora and the baby must leave. And they must leave today! Where they would go Joshua had absolutely no idea. He had a few savings that he had managed to make. It was not a fortune but it would be enough for them to survive for a short time until he found some work. He knew that his life here was over. He would never be able to return and he doubted he would see his Parents again! What would Flora say? How could he do this to the woman he loved? How had it all gone so horribly wrong?

Joshua knew that work could be found harvesting the fields in another part of Norfolk. He had heard some of the men from the village talking about it only the other week. Maybe he could get work there? How the hell did he find his way there? Where was the work? Joshua Bromfield did not have a clue. What he did know, however, was that he and his new family did not have any other choice. They would leave today. Surely their life elsewhere would be better than this? His only comforting thought was that he had a little money put aside and he was not afraid of hard work. He would work as hard as he could to make it up to Flora and the baby if it was the last thing he did!

As he came in sight of his house Joshua could see that Flora was standing at the window looking out for him. When she saw him approaching Flora ran to him and hugged him and the baby as though her life depended on it .Flora had been as good as her word and she had amassed as much of their belongings as she could. Joshua loaded the cart and together they left for their new life somewhere else in Norfolk. What sort of life it would be they could only guess at but, surely, it had to be a better life than they had here?

Chapter 7.

October 2012.

Pietre sat looking at copies of the birth certificates that fluttered in his shaking hands. The people mentioned in this document could be his relatives. Jessica Bromfield's birth and death had been registered in one part of Norfolk and then three short days later another birth had also been registered here at Saham Toney. Why had his long lost relatives been traveling with a new born child? Why had they decided to move so quickly?

 Pietre did not know the answers to this but what he did know was that it did not make sense. People were much less travelled then than they were today. Something major must have happened all those years ago to force his ancestors to move so far away from their previous home. What had happened to them? Why was a birth re-registered in Saham Toney after a birth and death had been registered elsewhere? Why did they move so far away? Whatever the reason Pietre sensed that he must try to find out. He was convinced that, if he discovered why, he would be one step closer to discovering another piece of the jigsaw. How could he find out any more information? Who did he know who could help him? Oscar Washington! Of course. Why had he not thought about him before? Pietre chided himself for his stupidity and resolved to contact the redoubtable Mr Washington as soon as the library at Thetford opened for business. With that idea planted firmly in his mind his thoughts drifted towards this afternoon. Maud had telephoned him to tell him that she had invited a couple of guests for dinner tonight if he didn't mind! How typical of Maud and Harold to consider his feelings like that. He was a guest in their daughter's house and yet they still felt it necessary to ask his permission. Pietre had grown incredibly fond of the older couple over the last few weeks and he was sure that, whoever the guests were, he would enjoy their company.

Gordon Jarvis was not entirely sure if he was going to enjoy this evening. How had he got to this? Maud and Harold Carrington had absolutely insisted that he and his beautiful future wife Mavis Riley join them for dinner that night. As Gordon thought about Mavis, his future wife no less, he allowed the beginnings of a smile to force itself into the corners of his mouth. After all he had been through over the last couple of years he still had to pinch himself when he realise the direction his life had taken. Mavis Riley, the redoubtable landlady of the local hostelry had agreed to be his wife! How the hell had that happened? How could he feel so happy and contented after all he had put himself and his family through? All Gordon did know was that Mavis made him feel alive again. She was like a breath of fresh air. When he had first come to the village he was a very different person to the genial host he was now. He had been racked with terrible guilt over the death of his first wife. His first wife! Why had he thought that? He had had only one wife and, when he had married, he thought that he would only ever have the one wife. So why had he just thought that? Why did he feel such ridiculous pleasure at the prospect of spending the rest of his life with the gorgeous, sexy, and vibrant Mavis? He knew that his life with Mavis would never be dull. He knew that she was a little minx who would try every way she knew how to get her own way. He knew all this and yet he didn't care! He was in love with Mavis Riley and he didn't care who knew it! Of course he was under no illusions that any of this was a secret in the village.

If the government could only harness the talents of the local residents to glean information out of anyone then they would have no need for M.I 5! As this thought crossed Gordon's mind he laughed out loud. Mavis came into the bedroom from the bathroom and smiled, indulgently, at her future Husband. "What's so funny my little Geordie gent? She asked good-naturedly.

Mavis Riley knew that she had struck gold a second time in her life. Her late Husband had been an absolute treasure to her but; she admitted only to herself, he had over- indulged her a little too much! She knew that, whilst Gordon loved her, he would not be so easily manipulated and that was something that she found deeply attractive.

She knew that their life together would not always be calm and smooth but, what the hell; didn't that make it all the more exciting?

"Should we take some wine with us Hinny? Or do you think that Maud and Harold will have sorted all that out?" The look that Mavis gave Gordon left him in no doubt that they should indeed take some wine with them and it must be the finest wine the pub had. It would not do to let the side down now would it?

As Gordon pulled into the driveway of "Haven's Retreat" it took all of his nerve not to turn the car around and flee. He remembered the time he spent at the house with the previous owners and all the amazing people he had met. He remembered all the good times but he would never forget the awful things that had happened to his new friends. As he nervously rang the front door bell Mavis gently linked his arm and gave his elbow a tiny squeeze. Mavis knew a little of what had gone on that summer and she also knew that, when the time was right, she would hear the rest of the story. But not tonight! Tonight was about enjoying the company of Harold and Maud and the rather handsome Pietre. Mavis had asked Maud outright if she had a crush on the gorgeous Pietre as she herself had admitted to finding him very easy on the eye! "Mavis Riley" Maud had exclaimed in mock indignation. "I'm sure I don't know what you mean."

Maud opened the door with a flourish and ushered them along the hall and into the lounge. As they passed the office Gordon was once again struck by the feeling of uncertainty and doubt that he had always had whenever he had passed the room. He had never spoken out about his irrational fears but, nevertheless, fear was what he felt whenever he thought about that room. He had only been into the room once and that was when the odious Burt had attempted to interrogate them about the missing Colonel Henderson. His thoughts were interrupted by the gentle prodding in his ribs by Mavis whose look told him to concentrate on what their hosts were saying or there would be serious trouble when they got home! How did women do that? How did women convey all that emotion and dismay with just one split second look? If he lived to be a thousand years old Gordon would never understand the complicated, exasperating but fantastic creatures known as women. And he had no intention of spending any more time thinking about that just now. Tonight he was going to enjoy himself and if he could exorcise a few ghosts concerning the history of the house –then that would not be a bad thing. Surely?

Mavis had told him that Pietre was in the process of discovering whether he was related to the original owners of the farmhouse and, he had had to admit to himself, he was more than a little interested in the house history too.

The evening was a great success. Maud had cooked a lovely meal for them all. "Not to your standards Mavis and Gordon" she had explained rather sheepishly "I would never attempt to compete with that fabulous Chef you have there." Both Mavis and Gordon had told Maud that the meal was simply delicious – which it was – and they had enjoyed themselves immensely. After the meal they all adjourned into the lounge where Harold had proceeded to ply them with drinks.

Pietre had been surprised when Gordon had told him that he had spent the summer living in the house and he seemed genuinely delighted that Gordon seemed interested in the house and its history. The only thing that had spoiled the evening for Gordon was when Maud, in her usual inimitable way, had insisted that they all go into the office and see what her Husband had produced. Mavis was inordinately proud of the accomplishments of her beloved husband Harold. Pietre had slowly and patiently instructed her Husband on the strange complexities of a computer. Harold Carrington had always had other people to look after that sort of thing when he was in the Army and he had never had the opportunity, or indeed the enthusiasm, to use a computer since. Pietre had told him to think of the computer as the enemy which had not been difficult and to use his undoubted prowess as a soldier to decide how best to defeat the said enemy. Harold had got the bit between his teeth and had startled and astounded himself by actually making a great deal of progress in a comparatively short time. Just wait until his Grandchildren got back from their vacation in Paris. They would not believe their eyes! Grandpa Harold on the computer!

Harold had stood to attention and escorted them all into the office. Was it just him or did anyone else feel the strange atmosphere in that room? Gordon had wondered as he looked around at the other people squashed into the tiny space. As his eyes passed over Pietre Gordon could have sworn he saw a fleeting glimpse of the same sort of concerns cross over Pieter's face. Don't be such an old fool Gordon had chided himself. Now he was just imagining all sorts of foolish things. Harold showed great delight in demonstrating what he had discovered on the computer. Oh! He fully realised that this sort of stuff was second nature to all you young folks but to Harold Carrington it was nothing short of a minor miracle.

As Harold continued to speak Pieter's thoughts began to concentrate themselves on this room. What was it about this room that he found so unsettling? Why did he feel nervous standing in this small crowded room? What was he to feel nervous or anxious about? Harold had managed to locate what he hoped would be some exciting information regarding his ancestors. He had been on the telephone to Oscar Washington at Thetford library where he had discovered the possibility that his long lost ancestors had moved from a different part of Norfolk. "I hope you don't mind Pietre but I took the liberty of telephoning Oscar Washington at Thetford and he was only too happy to help.

I know that you had said that you would ring him whenever you had the time but I just got the bit between my teeth and charged ahead. I do hope you are not offended dear boy. I was only trying to help" In the ensuing silence all the people in the room were wondering just what the matter with Pietre was! He did not seem aware of his surroundings. He did not seem aware of anyone else being in the room. He seemed both ill at ease and excited at the same time. Only Gordon seemed to be in tune with Pietre and he could not understand what was going on but he sensed it was something to do with this room and the distinct possibility that Pietre was connected to this house.

Pietre shook his head as if trying to dislodge his thoughts and he concentrated on the moment to hand. "What was that you were saying Harold? I was miles away! Sorry! Of course I don't mind you speaking to Oscar. It has saved me the time and trouble of doing it myself. So what theories did he come up with? If indeed he came up with any at all."

"Well", said Harold with barely disguised delight. "Oscar informed me that he thought it highly likely that Joshua Bromfield and his wife and child were the same people.

 It seemed inconceivable to Oscar that anyone with the exact same names and with a new born child could be different. Of course he realises that this is pure speculation but he was willing to bet his not inconsiderable reputation on it. So what do you think Pietre? Do you think that they are one and the same family? I do hope so as it will make our search considerably easier."

Pietre looked at the sea of expectant faces crowded into the office and smiled to himself. He hardly dared hope that this information as true because if it was then his search for answers was nearly over!

"Harold, I think you have been marvellous in what you have achieved in such a short time. I might have known that your Military background and your organisational skills would come in useful and, by golly, I think they have." As Pietre finished speaking he saw that both Maud and Mavis were struggling to keep a straight face. What had he done now he wondered? Just as he was about to ask what was so amusing - Maud spoke. "Oh Pietre, you really are so funny you know! I have never heard such a British saying such as "by golly" spoken with such a beautiful accent. You really do make me smile young man." Mavis giggled to herself as she eyed Pietre up with a coquettish smile. "Pietre you really are a delight! Your face was a picture of worry just a few moments ago and now you have the ability to make us all smile. How do you do it?" As Pietre looked around at his new found friends he could not help but notice that there was one person in the room who was not smiling. Gordon. As he caught his eye Gordon made a sterling effort to paint a beaming smile on his face but Pietre could not help but notice that the smile did not quite reach Gordon's eyes.

 As Pietre made his way upstairs at the end of the evening he could not get the image of Gordon's face out of his mind. What was troubling Gordon? Pietre knew that something was troubling him – but what? Pietre knew that he would have to speak to Gordon soon if he was to find out a little more about the house.

He had not told Harold and Maud, in fact he had only made up his mind that night, but he was going to head back to Sweden within the next few days. Pietre had decided to contact Sylvia Hendrickson again. He wasn't sure why but he did wonder if all this research into his lineage had unsettled him about his own future. He felt the need to think about settling down. Why had Sylvia gone off in such a hurry? Why had her Father reacted in such a strange way? These and many more questions filled Pieter's mind as he struggled to sleep.

Over in another part of the village several other people were struggling with sleep.

Elijah Stump knew he would not sleep that night. He knew that he must do something about the terrible nightmares he had been experiencing for the last few weeks. Elijah had lived here in the village all his life. He knew his parents, his grand-parents and his great grand-parents had lived here all their lives too. He had never had any desire to explore the outside world and he also knew why! Elijah Stump knew he was different from most other people. Elijah could both see and hear the dead! His "skill", such as it was, had never seemed that big a deal whilst he was a toddler but when he started to talk to his dead friends he un-nerved the local teacher so much that she called his Parents into school to discuss his sanity.

Elijah's parents were simple souls who had never benefitted from any regular sort of education as they had both lived on the outskirts of the village all their lives and had not been a part of village life at all. Elijah had often wondered just how different he was from other children. He did not make friend easily as he lacked any sort of social skills. He was quite happy talking to his "friends" all day. Lately, however, his friends had been anything other than friendly towards him. Elijah remembers the very moment he first set eyes on the blond stranger who had come to town to discover his ancestors. The instant he clapped eyes on him Elijah knew that he was someone who could cause him and his family trouble. Oh! He didn't know how exactly – he just knew. Over the next few weeks more and more of his "friends" had come to see him and whisper horrific things into his ear. They told him of the terrible things that would happen to him and his family if he didn't do the right thing about the stranger. What was the right thing? He didn't know and the voices just kept telling him the same thing. DO THE RIGHT THING!

As Elijah finally realised that sleep would once again elude him he clambered from the makeshift bed in the barn where he was currently living and wondered what to do.

Gordon Jarvis was also wondering what to do. He had enjoyed the majority of the night at the old farmhouse. Pietre seemed a really pleasant, intelligent and interesting man. What troubled Gordon was the fact that when he went into the office within the house he had caught Pietre looking at him as though he could read his mind. It was only the briefest of glances but Gordon knew that Pietre sensed something of his discomfort and although he had only just met Pietre Mortennson Gordon knew that he was unlikely to let anything rest until he had discovered all he could find about his ancestors. Why that should trouble him so much Gordon didn't know – what he did know was that, right now, all he wanted to do was go to sleep.

Gordon lay awake willing his thoughts to stay away from the awful events of the previous summer. To no avail! Gordon lay quietly beside his beloved Mavis and forced himself to remember. He remembered his first glimpse of the beautiful old farmhouse. He remembered how he had badly misjudged the redoubtable Prunella Okenden and he recalled the visit of Colonel Burt that ultimately caused the death of his young friend. What Gordon remembered most of all though was the indisputable feeling of evil he felt whenever he went into the office at the farmhouse! Gordon had never broached his concerns with Chris and Ronnie, the previous owners, but he somehow sensed that Chris felt something too. He had avoided that room as often as he could and since the new owners had arrived he had not had the need, or the inclination for that matter, to venture there again. What was it about that room that unsettled him so? He had always prided himself on his no nonsense approach to life. He had only ever believed in what he could see and in what he knew to be right. So why, in the darkness of the night, was he doubting himself. With a supreme effort he fought to banish these ridiculous thoughts. And so it was that Gordon Jarvis turned over and eventually fell into a dreamless sleep.

Elijah Stump, meanwhile, was not so fortunate.

The cool night air did nothing to settle Elijah's already frayed nerves. He often walked around the village in the early hours and, generally, this afforded him some level of peace. But not tonight. Tonight Elijah found no solace in his walk. Tonight he seemed to be not in charge of where he was walking. The "voices" in his head kept telling him to go to the farmhouse. Why? Elijah did not have the word power to express just what he "heard". It was not voices as such but a sense of being directed against his will. He had NEVER told a living soul that he did not feel in control of his own destiny. He knew that his Parents shared some of his talent (if you could call it a talent) but he also knew that he was different from them somehow. He rarely had any respite from their demands but recently it had become unbearable. He had not slept properly for weeks. He had not been able to eat properly for a long time and he was tired, very tired, of it all. Perhaps if he went to the farmhouse he would get better? He did not know what else to do. The "voices" in his head might just leave him alone if he did what they suggested. But did he have the nerve to do as they asked? Did he have it in him to kill the blond stranger in their midst? Would that end his nightmare as they had hinted? Would he finally be free? As these thoughts whirled around his brain Elijah Stump walk purposely toward the farmhouse.

At the gate that led to the house Elijah stopped and listened. The silence outside was complete. Apart from the birds and creatures that roamed the night there was not a sound. Elijah had always found comfort in this sort of silence – but not tonight. Suddenly a new voice filled his head. This was a woman's voice. This was a voice he had never heard before and, somehow, Elijah knew that whoever the voice belonged to was both excited and furious. Without stopping to think Elijah crept towards the farmhouse building. Elijah was stunned to see that he was not alone. Just in front of him stood the blond stranger. What the hell was he doing walking around at this time of night? What the hell was he supposed to do now? Quietly, and with terrible venom, the voice gave him his instructions and as Elijah Stump crept towards the man he KNEW what he must do.

Chapter 8.

Pietre slowly opened his weary eyes and looked around him. Where the hell was he? What was he doing lying in a strange bed? The last thing he remembered was walking around the garden at "Haven's Retreat" in the dead of the night! As he came too slowly Pietre also remembered a terrible pain at the back of his head and he gingerly brought his hand towards his neck before he heard a strange voice telling him not to move and she would go and fetch the Doctor. The Doctor! What did he need a Doctor for? And who was the woman walking purposefully away? Within seconds a face appeared before him and he saw a friendly, but concerned, face.

Doctor Brian Moseley looked directly at Pietre and forced a sort of smile. "How do you feel Mr Mortennson? No, please do not try to move. You are in Thetford General Hospital. Do you remember?"

Pietre looked at the kindly face in front of him and wondered what the hell was happening to him. He only knew that a few seconds ago he was standing in the garden and now he was looking at a total stranger and he had the worst headache he had ever had!

Doctor Moseley then proceeded to examine Pietre carefully. He took his pulse, he shone a blinding light into Pieter's eyes and he gently began to remove the bandage from around Pieter's head. A bandage that Pieter didn't even know was wrapped around his head! What the hell was going on?

"Sorry! What did you just say? The Police want to talk to me as soon as I feel ready! What do the Police want to speak to me about? Will someone please tell me what the hell is going on?"

A movement at the side of the bed caught Pieter's eye and he finally recognised a face. Maud Carrington looked so troubled that Pietre began to be worried – very worried. Maud had obviously been crying and he could see that it was taking a lot out of her not to burst into tears again. "Oh my dear boy! How do you feel? We have all been so terribly worried about you for the last 2 weeks. We all prayed that you would recover. The vicar, Harold, My daughter and her family and especially myself, have all been praying night and day for some sort of miracle and now it has happened." With that Maud dissolved into tears and turned to someone just out of Pieter's sight. Slowly Harold Carrington came into view and Pieter could see that he looked a worried man.

"So glad to see you awake young man. You gave us all a fright I don't mind telling you! Now you must promise me that you will take it easy and rest. The Doctor's seem to think that you should make a full recover. Thank god. But you must rest. Promise me that you will do as the Doctor says?"

Pieter could not take this all in. What the hell was everyone going on about? Why did he need to rest? What was he doing in Thetford General? Why did his head hurt? As Pietre struggled to make any sort of sense of what was going on Doctor Moseley spoke.

"Pietre, you have sustained a very nasty head injury. You have been unconscious for two weeks during which time we have endeavoured to reduce the swelling on your brain. I realise that all of this must come as a great shock to you but, let me assure you, we all believe that, now you have regained consciousness, you should, with time, make a full recovery. Now I am going to give you a sedative which will enable you to relax. Your brain took quite a beating and we need to ensure that you are stable before we even consider moving you into another ward. Do you understand Mr Mortennson?"

Pietre did not understand. He did not understand at all! All he wanted to do was to get out of bed and go home but his legs would not do as they were told! Why did his legs not move? Slowly and inexorably Pietre surrendered to the warm safety of sleep.

"Oh! Harold! I can't believe that he has come round after all this time. I have prayed and prayed for this. Oh thank you Lord!"

Harold Carrington put his arm protectively around his beloved wife and made suitable soothing sounds but his own mind was still in turmoil. Pietre looked dreadful but the Doctors were optimistic of his recovery. So what next? Harold had not been able to stop thinking about the motive for such a senseless and cowardly attack. The Police seem to think that it wasn't a robbery that had gone tragically wrong. Pietre had not been carrying anything of value. So why was Pieter attacked? Was it that he had disturbed a potential robbery after all? If so then the Police did not seem to be taking this as seriously as he had hoped. The local Constable had been professional but ineffective when Harold had asked him for his opinion. Why would anyone try to cave in Pieter's head like that? The weapon used had not been found. A motive had not been established and so the local Constabulary had decided that Pieter just happened to be in the wrong place at the wrong time!

Harold was far from convinced about that but he was also unsure of what to do next. He had grown inordinately fond of the young man lying in the bed- even though they had known each other a comparatively short time- and he vowed that, somehow, he would get to the bottom of this mystery if it was the last thing he ever did!

Elijah Stump was a worried man. He could not quite believe what he had done. He had crept up behind the blond man and he had hit him HARD. Very hard - with the first thing he had laid his hands on. He looked with utter disgust at the brick he held in his trembling hand. The blood had started to darken and congeal and he realised, with absolute horror, that the brick had some matted hair on it! What had he done? What had possessed him to do it? When that thought entered, uninvited, into his head he knew what had possessed him. Or rather he sensed what had possessed him. Lately the strongest voice crowding into his brain had kept repeating the same thing over and over again! He had refused to believe what he was hearing at first but the voice would not let him rest. She kept saying that the stranger was responsible for her own death nearly 200 hundred years before! How could that man be responsible? What the hell did she mean? The voice continued to haunt his every waking hour. It was incessant. It was terrifying. For days before he had not slept properly. He had not eaten. He had tried, so hard, to ignore that voice until he could stand it no longer.

He had weakened and she had seized on his weakness with a hunger and hatred that had completely overwhelmed him. Elijah did not know precisely when he had lost his mind completely. What he did realise now though was that he was in real trouble. He had always been an outsider. He had always been someone whom the local community distrusted and feared. He also knew, without a doubt, that certain people in the village would put two and two together. Elijah Stump lay down on the makeshift bed in the old barn and waited to be found. He had no strength left to fight. He was exhausted. It was if the voice inside his head had drained every last ounce of his strength and resolve. There was no way out for him now. He shuddered at the thought of going to prison for this. He could not let that happen to him. He would die in prison. He would lose what little grasp he had on reality if he went there. What should he do? Her voice inside his head had been strangely quiet since his terrible act of violence and he hoped that she would leave him alone now. But somehow he doubted that.

He knew that she wouldn't stay silent for long and he really couldn't bear another moment of this torture. So Elijah knew what he had to do. Slowly he rose from his bed and went out. If he was dead then the voices would stop. If he was dead then no-one could put the blame on him. Oh! They would have their suspicions. People always had their suspicions! But they could not prove it was him. Could they? Elijah looked once again at the blood soaked brick and made his mind up. Step by slow step he retraced his steps into the house where his Parent's lived. He crept silently to a large cupboard and unlocked it. His Parents did not know that he had a key to the gun cupboard. They had never let him near it before. Elijah allowed himself a brief smile as he recalled how he had managed to steal the key for the afternoon and have a copy made. He had enjoyed shooting small animals and watching them as they slowly died. It had been his only pleasure for such a long time. Elijah also knew what to do to ensure a quick and relatively painless death.

Elijah Stump went back out of the house as quietly as he had entered and never looked back. When he arrived at his special place within the forest he carefully loaded the rifle, put the barrel in his mouth, closed his eyes and began to pull the trigger!

Chapter 9.

Pietre was kept in hospital for 10 days and, despite the protestations of his Doctor, had discharged himself. He had promised to see the local Doctor and Nurse if anything untoward happened and he smiled to himself as he remembered the determination etched on the faces of both Harold and Maud who, almost in unison, had declared that the young man standing sheepishly in front of them would not be allowed to get away with anything if they had anything to do with it.

Pietre sat at the desk in his bedroom at "Haven's Retreat" and looked at the patterns being created by the sun shining through the trees. It was a beautiful, peaceful vista but in his heart Pietre was feeling opposite emotions. As he looked at the photocopy of another marriage certificate from 1828 he was wondering just where this story would end. In the weeks that had followed since his release from hospital he had enjoyed the continuing hospitality of both sets of Carrington's. Gerry and Elspeth had insisted that he continued to live with them at the farmhouse. After all hadn't they got enough room now that Thomas was here and there at Catering College and Grace was always sleeping over at some friend or another and, besides, Maud and Harold would never forgive them for throwing him out onto the street! As he thought of Maud and Harold he was, once again, bowled over by the sheer generosity and stamina of his friends. They had continued his research into his genealogy with outstanding energy and drive. If he lived to be their age he hoped he had half of their get up and go. They had discovered some pretty unusual things which, although at times very tenuous, did seem to follow the trail of his recent ancestors back to Joshua and Flora Bromfield who were not present on the previous census but did appear in the one dated 1810.

Pietre had mentioned this to Oscar Washington at Thetford library and had asked his opinion about the possibility of them being a distant relative. Oscar had been over the moon at the prospect of researching for him. Oscar had, as usual, been a marvel. It had taken him several days; he had apologised profusely and had embarrassed himself by admitting that he had done a lot of the research in "company time" something he hoped that Pietre would not inform his employers about! It was Oscar's belief that Joshua and Flora Bromfield were more than likely the same couple who had registered their marriage in another part of the County. Oscar also told him that it was quite unusual for people to travel very far at that time as work was hard to come by and most people tended to live in the same village for all their lives. Many times, sometimes going back several generations, the same family could be traced back fairly easily.

Pieter's thoughts returned to the copy of the document in his hand. Saturday 1st September 1810.

The census for that year showed that a man, his wife and young daughter were now living in Saham Toney. This, in itself, was not exceptional and might have gone unnoticed if it wasn't for the keen eye of Oscar Washington! Oscar, it seemed, had taken up Pieter's quest for information about his family with fervent relish and he had been as certain as he could be that the new people were in fact his long lost family.

As Oscar had gone on to explain that the names, whilst not being unusual, were the same as they had discovered previously. They were the right age and they had not appeared on the previous census of the area. It was Oscar's opinion that they were indeed one and the same family. Of course he could not guarantee this but as Oscar had said the day before – he would stake his not inconsiderable reputation on it! Pietre smiled to himself as he remembered the look of embarrassment on Oscar's face as he realised that that last statement sounded more than a little pompous in his own words. Everyone had assured him that his reputation was second to none and of course they realised that it was not an exact science when the paper trail was so difficult but they all thought that he was correct in his considered opinion. Oscar had agreed to continue his forensic genealogy as he grandly put it and would be in touch the very second he had anything to report!

So, if the people on this census were indeed his ancestors, why had they come to Saham Toney? Why here of all places? Why? Why? Why? Pietre, at this stage, did not have any answers. What he did have though, and this sounded bizarre even to himself, was that he somehow KNEW that he was connected to Joshua, Flora and Jessica. He could not rationalise this and he could hardly explain it to himself but he knew, with unwavering certainty that he was on the right track.

Chapter 10.

February 1811.

Jessica Bromfield woke early that morning. Even earlier than usual. As the first, tentative, rays of wintry sunshine struggled to make themselves known that frosty morning Jessica got out of her little cot at the end of her Mummy and Daddy's bedroom and toddled determinedly towards her sleeping Parent's. Even at such an early age Jessica had shown a remarkable understanding of "moods" and "atmosphere's" around the house. Both Joshua and Flora were aware of this and were not a little worried. Their beloved Daughter had second sight! There could be no doubt. Hadn't they attempted to dismiss their employers concerns many times that their little daughter just had a vivid imagination and all her "little friends" that she spoke to were just her imagination? Her employers had accepted this at first but both Joshua and Flora were not convinced that this situation would last forever! As Jessica tugged at the bedclothes to ensure that her Parent's woke up no-one could have predicted the events that would unfold before the end of the day.

"Mamma, Papa, wake up. It's my special day! It's my birthday. Wake up! As sleep deserted both of them they looked at their beautiful child's expectant face and any lingering doubts were erased. Their Daughter's command of language was exceptional. Their Daughter was exceptional. Today was going to be a very special day. They had arranged for all of them to go for a lovely walk that afternoon as they had the afternoon off from work. Mr and Mrs Weaver, the farm owners, had quickly agreed that as it was Jessica's birthday they could both have the afternoon off as long as all the work was done and that Flora would be back for evening milking. Just think thought Flora. A whole afternoon off! How good would that be? The weather was bright and cold as they set off for their walk. The morning had been busy for them all and Jessica had done everything she could do to help. Her little girl was so excited about her birthday! Joshua had carved a little doll out of a spare piece of wood and Flora had recycled one of her old working skirts to make a dress for the doll. It was simple and unsophisticated but Jessica had been delighted with her gift and had proceeded to show everyone her gift at every opportunity. Mr and Mrs Weaver had indulged Jessica as she was such a ray of sunshine. That little girl would brighten up any day Mrs Weaver had said on numerous occasions over the time that the family had worked for them. As they continued to walk around the small pond in the centre of the village Jessica ran on ahead. Suddenly she stopped running, sat down and began talking to her doll. At least that was what both her Parent's thought as they came towards their precious little girl. "What are you telling Dolly Jessica? Are you telling her all about your lovely birthday? Have you told her that if you are a really good girl you will be having a special Birthday tea? As Flora's words left her mouth she caught sight of Jessica's face. It was contorted into a terrible grimace and she was moaning and muttering to herself. "What are you saying Jessica? Mamma can't understand what you are saying? Tell me sweetheart!" At the sound of her Mother's voice Jessica froze. Joshua and Flora stopped dead in their tracks at the malevolent look that crossed Jessica's face. "What is it my Darling girl? What's the matter? Are you alright? Come here darling – come to Papa." The next words that they heard would haunt them until their dying day. "Mamma, Papa who is Lizzie Stump?"

Flora did not know what to say or do. Suddenly the sunshine deserted the sky. Suddenly the whole world began to sway and Flora hit the ground hard as she fainted!

As she slowly came round Flora could hear the sound of Jessica crying and her Husband's voice as he attempted, rather unsuccessfully, to calm their little girl down. With a supreme effort Flora sat up and tried to assure her little girl that she would be fine just as soon as they all got home and they all had that special birthday tea that they had promised Jessica.

Both Joshua and Flora thought that the day would never end but, at last, Jessica was tucked up in bed cuddling her new doll which she had vehemently insisted was to be called Lizzie!

Joshua was the first to break the dreadful silence that had descended on them both as they lay in bed listening to the soft breathing of their precious girl. "Flora, my love. Are you awake? "Joshua already knew the answer but he was trying his level best to avoid having this conversation. The sound of Flora's tears almost broke his heart but Joshua knew that, somehow, he must find the strength again to face the prospect of Lizzie Stump still being part of their lives!

As dawn made its first tentative steps on the day both Joshua and Flora were exhausted. They had talked all night. They had talked and talked but had not come up with any other solution to their problem but the one that neither of them wanted to happen.

They must tell Jessica all about Lizzie and the "voices" that she hears. Just how to explain to such a little girl all about "second sight" they had absolutely no idea - but she needed to know if she was to remain safe and out of danger.

Jessica Bromfield sat and listened as her Parent's tried to explain all about Lizzie Stump. They tried to explain that Lizzie wasn't real. They tried to explain so many different things to her. Jessica knew that Lizzie wasn't "real". She, somehow, knew that other little children were not like she was. What Jessica did know, though, was that she had a gift. Her Parent's thought of it as a curse but she knew differently. Jessica was only 4 years old but her psychic ability far exceeded that of both of her Parent's. She could not explain how it happened but she knew that she could "see" people that others couldn't. This fact did not upset her because she had ALWAYS been able to see like this. She saw Lizzie Stump as clearly as she saw her own Parent's. What Jessica did not realise though was the influence that Lizzie was having over her. Lizzie was such fun! Lizzie was always making her laugh! Lizzie always talked about them both going away on a great adventure! Lizzie said that soon her niece would come to pay a visit. It would probably be when her Mummy and Daddy were at work but that wouldn't matter would it? This nice lady would take Jessica on a fabulous adventure but it was a secret! No-one must know. No-one must guess what fun they would have. All Jessica had to do was to go with Lizzie's niece when she arrived and she wasn't to make a sound. Could Jessica do that? Asked Lizzie. Of course she could, thought Jessica. She might only be 4 but she could keep a secret! Especially one that involved an adventure!

Flora sat quietly watching her beloved Daughter. Jessica was so young! How could she possibly comprehend what they had just said?

Both she and Joshua could hardly comprehend it themselves. As she continued to watch Jessica Flora sensed, rather that saw, a presence in the room. She glanced nervously at Joshua. His barely imperceptible nod in her direction was just enough to tell her that he sensed it too. What was going on? What would happen next? Suddenly the atmosphere in the room changed. The air became heavy with a terrible sense of foreboding. Quietly at first Jessica began to chant. Neither Flora nor Joshua knew what was going on or what was being chanted but they instinctively knew that, whatever was happening, something was wrong! Slowly, but inexorably, Jessica's voice began to change. It became lower in pitch. It became more and more incoherent until she was not making any sense to her bewildered and frightened Parent's. Suddenly the door to their cottage burst open and a young woman burst in chanting the same sounds that little Jessica was making. Without a glance in their direction the young woman snatched Jessica from in front of them and started for the door. Flora screamed with all her might and Joshua ran towards his Daughter but stopped, appalled, at the sight that beheld him. His beloved Jessica's face was contorted into a mask of unbelievable horror. Her very features began to resemble another person. Someone Joshua hoped he would never have to see again. As he stood, transfixed, a terrible sound emanated from his beautiful Daughter's body.

The stranger began to sway and chant. Jessica began to sway and chant. The air in the room became stiflingly oppressive and malevolent. Then Jessica turned her head towards her horrified Parent's and laughed- but this laugh lacked any vestige of humour. Jessica began to convulse violently as the stranger gripped her ever tighter. Suddenly Lizzie Stumps voice filled the room. How could that be? Lizzie Stump was dead! Joshua Bromfield had killed her! Hadn't he? Lizzie's voice became louder and louder until the noise was unbearable. With cold, unbelieving, certainty both Flora and Joshua realised that Lizzie's voice was coming from the tiny body of their 4 year old Daughter!

The next few moments would live in all their memories forever. Joshua Bromfield might have killed the physical body of Lizzie Stump but he had not been able to kill her evil spirit. What Lizzie's spirit, or indeed anyone else for that matter, had not anticipated was the depth of love a Mother has for her child. Flora Bromfield did not know that she had it in her. All she knew was that she had to protect her family at all costs. Flora assailed the stranger holding her Daughter with the first thing that came to hand!

The long handled razor sharp kitchen knife made short work of the stranger.

Flora continued to hack away at her body long after the girl had left this mortal earth. It had taken all of Joshua's strength to prise her away from the body. Jessica, meanwhile, had been unnervingly quiet during the terrible onslaught happening before her young eyes.

Chapter 11.

June 1828.

Jessica lay quietly in her bed savouring the moment. It was just after dawn and, already, the sun was coming over the horizon with a promise of another glorious day. As she lay looking out of the window down to the garden she smiled inwardly. Today was her wedding day! As she languished in her bed Jessica's thoughts involuntarily went back to the time they had first arrived in the village. Her dear, beloved, Parent's had never mentioned the tragic and awful events that had made them flee. Over the years Jessica had grown into a beautiful, confident and dutiful Daughter one whom any Parent would be proud of. Except for one thing! Jessica had never again mentioned her "gift" to anyone. She had realised just how potentially dangerous her "gift" could be. Very few people had the dubious ability to see and talk to dead people.

As the years rolled on and her Parent's had made a new and successful life here in the village NO-ONE had any notion that the Bromfield's were anything other than a decent hard working family and Jessica would not be the one to tell them any different!

Today she was going to become Mrs Benjamin Smythson. Today was the beginning of a new chapter in her life and she could hardly wait! As she lay there Jessica bathed in the early morning sun and felt almost completely contented. Almost – but not quite. She climbed out of bed and shook her head as if to try and dislodge the feelings she had. Today would NOT end in tragedy and heartbreak despite what all the voices in her head had been warning her of for the last few months. Today was going to be absolutely perfect from dawn to dusk if she and her redoubtable Parents had anything to do with it. As she thought of her Parent's Jessica's mind wandered back again over the years since they had arrived in Saham Toney when she had been 4 years old. The horror of what she had witnessed had abated over the years but Jessica could visualise every minute detail as if it had been etched onto her brain. They had left the farmhouse that Jessica had called home for all her life that fateful evening. She had been bundled into the back of a handcart and had been sworn to absolute silence. In truth Jessica was still in a state of total shock. She had witnessed her beloved Father slaughtering two women and her own Mother had hacked a complete stranger to death in front of her!

Her Mother had packed most of their belongings into the handcart and they had travelled for several days – each time sleeping in the handcart away from any people – until they had arrived at Saham Toney. Her Father had secured himself some work on the land and, over time, her Mother had started to work for the biggest local Landowner as a seamstress. As the years went on the Bromfield's settled into village life and became an integral part of the community. The only thing that the community did not know about was the reason for the sudden arrival of the strangers in their midst. Some of the villagers had been curious at first but Jessica never knew just what her Parent's had said about this but, eventually, people did not ask anymore. The one thing that had hardly been discussed was Jessica's "gift". Jessica had astounded her Parent's by insisting that they talk about it.

She may have been only 4 years old but the complexity and depth of Jessica' amazing skills made it impossible for her Parent's to ignore! As the years went by Jessica realised just how different she was from other children. This never bothered her as she had become very adept at hiding her "skill". She "saw" people all day every day. She heard them speak. She saw them going about their daily lives. She also saw that, with the exception of her Parent's – whose ability was much more limited than hers – no-one in the village could see or hear what she could see or hear!

As she sat at her dressing table brushing her hair ready for her wedding day Jessica laughed out loud at her first memory of a "ghost". She had stood quietly in the corner of the school yard discreetly watching this new girl pulling faces and making rude noises right beside some of the other pupils. Jessica wondered what the matter with the other children was. If someone had been making fun of them like this new girl was she would have had something to say!

Suddenly the new girl walked straight towards the group of schoolchildren and walked right through them! Jessica had cried out at this and several children standing close by looked shocked and uncomfortable. As Jessica looked up she was surprised to see the new girl wave at her and start to walk towards her! Jessica did not fancy the idea of someone walking straight through her and so she began to run towards the schoolhouse. Within a split second the new girl was at her side pleading with her to talk to her as she was so lonely.

That was the beginning of a lifelong friendship between Jessica and Mary. Over the years the friendship had changed. Jessica, of course, had aged but Mary was still a young girl of 5. Eventually Jessica had left the school and Mary had only occasionally visited her at home. The first time this had happened Jessica was troubled. She was worried about Mary and how she would get back to school. Mary had laughed and told her not to worry! She would be safe. After all she was already dead wasn't she? As Mary said that Jessica realised the seriousness of her situation! She was having a relationship with a dead schoolgirl! When she told her Parent's about this her Parent's reaction had frightened and dismayed her. They had talked about removing Jessica from school and for her to be taught at home! Jessica did not want this and it took all her powers of persuasion to convince her Parent's that she would be fine at school after all. That was the beginning of Jessica hiding the true level of her skills from her beloved Mother and Father. As the years went by and her skills were never mentioned it was almost as if they never existed.

Jessica was brought out of her reverie by the sound of her Mother's gentle voice asking her if she was awake.

Flora Bromfield watched her beautiful Daughter as she continued to brush her long golden blonde hair. She looked beautiful today. Of course she always would look beautiful to her but she looked positively radiant this morning. Flora hoped with every fibre of her being that Jessica would have a wonderful life with Benjamin whom she had grown to love and admire. Despite her best efforts to the contrary Flora could not help this niggling doubt from creeping back into her sub-conscious. Would Jessica have a wonderful life? Could she be truly happy? Did Benjamin have any inclination about Jessica's "gift"?

Why did this awful feeling of dread and fear keep threatening to overcome her? Nothing would spoil this magical day – surely?

As Joshua walked Jessica down the aisle of their local church in Saham Toney nobody noticed as a stranger slipped quietly into church and watched from a discreet distance as Miss Jessica Bromfield became Mrs Benjamin Smythson.

Arthur Stump was a stranger to Saham Toney. He was not, however, a stranger to Joshua and Flora Bromfield! He doubted if either of them would recognise or even realise the connection. He had found the dismembered bodies of his Aunt and Great Aunt just moments after their slaughter. He had stood aghast in the kitchen as he took in the carnage surrounding him and he had sworn that day that he would avenge the memory of his Aunt by finding the person who had done this to his family and ensuring that vengeance was his!

He was 10 years old! He had not been able to save the body of Lizzie Stump but he had been able to save her spirit.

As he sat cradling the disfigured and bloody body of his Aunt Lizzie he had had the strangest feeling. If he didn't know any better he would have sworn that his own body was slowly being taken over by Lizzie! How stupid did that sound? It couldn't be happening? Surely!

As the years went on Arthur struggled to separate his own thoughts from the whisperings of his Aunt Lizzie. Every day he would be bombarded with vitriol from Lizzie. She was consumed by her hatred for the Bromfield's and slowly and inexorably Arthur became Lizzie in thought and deed. Oh! He might have had the outer appearance of a young man but inside, in the very darkest recesses of his psyche, he was Lizzie Stump!

Arthur Stump realised with a jolt that the marriage service was over and the guests were making their way to the farmhouse that Joshua and Flora had had built for the newly married Mr and Mrs Smythson. As Arthur mingled with the other guests he began to form a plan. In truth Lizzie began to form a plan. How could she exact vengeance on the Bromfield's to avenge the heinous crimes inflicted on her family? The irony of the situation was completely lost on both Lizzie and Arthur.

As he entered the new farmhouse he was amazed that absolutely no-one stopped him front walking straight through the front door! Did they have no idea who he was? Did they not even care?

Suddenly Arthur's vision was assailed by Jessica and Benjamin as they came into the entrance hall. She looked radiant and he looked to be so proud that, for a moment at least, Arthur's determination wavered. Could he really do this? Could he really do what his Aunt Lizzie was asking him? NO! Not asking – demanding!

Just as Jessica and Benjamin walked passed Arthur realised that both Joshua and Flora were right beside them. Suddenly Arthur's breathing became more laboured. Suddenly he was not in full control of his mind and his body.

Suddenly his conscious thoughts were bombarded with Lizzie Stump's voice screaming at him that now was the time! Now was the time! Now was the time!!!

As if in slow motion Arthur Stump walked up to the newly wedded couple to offer his congratulations. As he reached out to kiss the bride Arthur noticed that Joshua Bromfield was shouting out. Arthur noticed that Flora was crying, Arthur noticed that Benjamin was trying to push him away. Arthur did not notice, however, the knife in his hand; Arthur did not notice the knife slicing into Flora's chest. He did not notice that the hallway was on fire as he had stumbled and crashed into the hearth and various ornaments etc. had fallen to the ground and begun to burn. Arthur did not notice that Joshua was pushing him to the ground all the time screaming for him to stop! For God's sake stop! Arthur did not notice the knife slice through Joshua's eye and embed itself into his brain. Arthur did not notice any of this. Lizzie Stump, however, noticed it all. Lizzie Stump smiled to herself as she noted that her lifelong, or should that be death long? , ambition had been realised!

Chapter 12.

Jessica Smythson stood silently looking at the bodies of her Parents. She stood immobile and silent as events went on around her. Everyone was either screaming or trying desperately to hold on to the man who had just brutally murdered her Parents on her wedding day! She never noticed that the man responsible had a knife at the throat of one of the Guests and was backing out of the house. She did not realise that the man had made his escape. All she could see was the mutilated bodies of her beloved Parents as they lay lifeless before her! She became aware of the noise before she fully realised that the terrible sound was her own voice as she became completely hysterical. Jessica allowed herself to be dragged off her Parents prostrate bodies by Benjamin and a few other guests.

For the next few days Jessica went around in a silent stupor. No-one could get through to her – not even her beloved new Husband. She neither ate nor slept and she violently refused to allow anyone to take off her blood stained wedding dress.

 She could not bear the thought of ever taking that dress off! If she took the dress off then it was true that her Parents were dead! It was true that she had witnessed this terrible thing!

Eventually Benjamin had no option but to call in the Doctor as he and his Parents become so concerned with Jessica's mental state that they all feared for her sanity and her life. Jessica Smythson fought like an alley cat to try to prevent herself from being sedated. She clawed and screamed at her new Husband as he and the Doctor administered the sedative. As she slowly and inevitably succumbed to the effects of the drug Benjamin Smythson did not know what to do next. The Doctor told him that his new Wife would be sedated for at least the next six hours. Six hours to decide what the hell to do! As he looked around the devastation he realised that they could no longer contemplate living her at the farm. He doubted that Jessica would be able to bear it. He could not bear the thought himself. Benjamin was a decent, hardworking and devoted man who was completely out of his depth right now, but what he instinctively knew was, if they were going to survive this terrible ordeal, they needed to get away from here. They needed to get as far away from here as was possible!

It took Benjamin a week to complete the arrangements. During that time Jessica had remained in a state of flux. Her Doctor had continued to administer the sedation and, eventually, Jessica had stopped putting up such a desperate fight to prevent this happening.

The funeral of his Parents-in –law had taken place within the week. Jessica had attended but did not appear to realise what was happening. Benjamin became increasingly concerned for the mental state of his beloved Wife. She was sedated, he knew that, but he realised that she was retreating within herself with every passing minute and he could not bear the thought of that! Benjamin was a good business man – a very good business man – who had contacts all over the country and beyond. He made the difficult decision to move to Sweden without consulting his Parents or indeed anyone remotely close to them both. Why he did not know but he sensed that if anyone in the village knew where they were heading then all of this horrific business would follow them and they would never be free!

He had listened aghast as several villagers had recounted tales of witchcraft etc. Witchcraft! He was, at first, completely sceptical but slowly and inexorably doubts began to invade his mind. Could this be true? Could any or all of it be true? All Benjamin knew for sure was they needed to escape and they needed to escape right now!

As he packed the last of their belongings into the carriage Benjamin looked back at the beautiful new farmhouse that his generous in-laws had given them as a wedding gift he wondered just what their lives could have been like there. He had serious misgivings that he was doing the right thing by leaving for Sweden so quickly but he also realised that it would be impossible to live in that house after the awful events of that terrible day. He had been both surprised and delighted to have realised that the farmhouse had attracted a great deal of interest when he had suggested selling up. How anyone could bear to live in that house was beyond him but, if someone was willing to buy it, he would gladly sell up and never set foot in the village or, indeed, the country again! Benjamin was a quietly ambitious man who adored his beautiful but traumatised wife with all his heart and he would do anything and everything to make her happy. How she would react to the news that they would be living in a different country he was not sure, but surely, anywhere they lived would be better than this surely?

Jessica sat impassively in exactly the same place that he had tenderly left her. She had not uttered a single word since the awful events of the previous week and he had listened to the various Doctors who had all agreed that, perhaps, it was the right thing to do to remove Jessica from the farmhouse as quickly as possible. No-one would guarantee that this would help at all but he had to do something! Right?

As the coach drew away from "Haven's Retreat" Jessica Smythson seemed completely unaware of what was happening around her. She looked up with vacant eyes as her Husband gently placed a travel rug over her knees and tenderly held her hand. Today was the start of their new life together and Benjamin prayed with every bone in his body that he was doing the right and proper thing. Only time would tell!

Chapter 13.

Pietre sat quietly, or should that be forlornly, at London's Heathrow airport. He sat with his laptop unopened on his lap. How appropriate was the term laptop eh? Thought Pietre with only a little sense of bitter irony. Since his "accident" almost a month ago his mood had struggled to get past belligerent! Would he ever be the same easy going guy he had been in his youth thought Pietre? As this thought ambushed him it took all of Pietre Mortenson's considerable resolve not to burst into hysterical laughter! Whenever had he been easy going? Whenever had he been a teenager? Whenever was he going to forgive his so called Parent's for having the temerity to die and leave him all alone and lonely in this hard world?

As these thoughts crowded into the little space left in his thoughts Pieter's mind strayed to the real reason he was going back to Sweden. Oh! He had tried his best to convince Maud, Harold, Elspeth and Gerry that he needed some time for rest and recuperation in his own country for a little while but he was absolutely convinced that no-one at "Haven's Retreat" had believed a single word! Maud Carrington had fixed him with what he called her "death stare" and forced him to admit that all this delving into his genealogy had made him curious about his immediate past? He had denied it categorically of course but he had succumbed to Maud's "death stare" and admitted that he needed to go back to Sweden "just to finish off a little bit of business".

As he walked towards the aircraft Pietre Mortenson would not admit, even to himself, just how nervous he really was. What would he find in Sweden? Would he find what he wanted or would he be heartbroken? What would his next move be? All these conflicting thoughts and emotions threaten to overwhelm Pietre as he slowly hobbled his way to his seat.

As the 'plane touched down in Stockholm Pietre was in a more benevolent mood. He had taken the flight time to reflect on his journey so far. He had started out, initially, with an idle curiosity of his real lineage. Not an idle curiosity! An overwhelming curiosity! If he wasn't going to end up cheating himself then Pietre knew that he must be totally honest with himself about the real motivation behind his quest.

Sylvia Hendrickson.

Sylvia Hendrickson.

She was the real reason he was heading back to Stockholm. She was the reason he was going back to arrange a visit with her father. Mr Hendrickson the Chief Executive of Hendrickson International Corporation. With a jolt Pietre suddenly realised that he didn't even know the first name of the father of his one true love! Oh God! How mawkish does that sound thought Pietre as he unfastened his seat belt. It might sound mawkish but it was closer to the truth than Pietre was prepared to admit!

At the airport Pietre was met by the private detective whom he had employed in his initial search for his ancestry. This time, however, the detective's skills had been brought to bear on a different tack. Finding the whereabouts of Sylvia Hendrickson!

It had been almost 18 months since Sylvia had called a halt to their burgeoning romance but in all that time Pietre had never really considered what Sylvia might be doing right now! What if she was engaged? What if she was married? What the hell would he do then?

As he settled into the back seat of his limousine Pietre thought, perhaps for the first time, that being so wealthy could actually be to his advantage! What was the use of all this money if he couldn't make it work for him?

Within 24 hours of arriving back at home in Sweden Pietre had set up a meeting with the head of the Hendrickson International Corporation. Why had Pietre said to himself that now he was home he would set up the meeting? Where was home after all? Surely not Sweden? If not Sweden then where else could he call home? Saham Toney?

Pietre Mortenson had always prided himself on adhering to the philosophy of "wherever I lay my hat, that's my home!" but now he wasn't quite so sure! (What was the name of that English singer who had the hit with that song title?)

Tomorrow he was due to meet with the President of the Company. Maybe now he would get some answers. So why did he feel it necessary to conceal his identity? What had the President got to hide? What advantage did Pieter hope to gain from the element of surprise? What the hell was he supposed to do next? As all these thoughts, and many more uninvited ones, crowded his brain Pietre Mortenson could never have predicted just how tomorrow would work out!

Chapter 14.

As Pietre walked towards the imposing, and not a little intimidating, Head Office of the Hendrickson Corporation he was still deciding the best course of action. He knew that Sven Hendrickson might just recognise him immediately and call the meeting off- after all he had turned and walked away from him without a backward glance the first, and only, time they had met. If he did call off the meeting Pietre was not sure what his next move might be but he knew that he had come too far to back out now! The detective had been of some help in researching the history of the Hendrickson Corporation and his findings had astounded Pietre!

The Company had been formed at the same time as his own Parent's. He had discovered that his Parent's and Sven Hendrickson had at one time been partners in another logistics Company before their apparent decision to go their separate ways. What had happened to make them split up a very profitable Company like that? Why did his Parent's never mention to him the connection between the two Companies? How many times had he argued with his Father about his decision not to come into the family firm? How they had argued about his Father's decision not to accept the almost ludicrous amount of money Hendrickson had offered to take over his Father's business? Pietre had always thought his Father had been too proud, stubborn or just plain foolish not to accept what was an amazing offer!

What the Detective had stumbled upon during his research had appalled Pietre. He had discovered that there had been rumours regarding financial misappropriation of Company funds by his Father! Nothing had ever been proven but the allegations had been voiced in the Financial Section of the local paper and this had been picked up by the National Press as the Company was a very successful enterprise and there was even talk of floating the Company on the Stock Exchange! Pietre had had absolutely no idea of any of this and so he had asked the Detective to dig deeper. The results had disappointed Pietre. No further evidence had surfaced and he had come to a dead end. However Pietre was not convinced and he had decided to speak to Hendrickson about this. He had set up the meeting on the pretext of giving logistic work to the Corporation for his own Company. He had surmised, quite rightly, that the prospect of a multi-million dollar Contract would interest Sven Hendrickson and so a meeting had been set up for 2pm that afternoon.

The Detective had also found out that Sylvia Hendrickson had gone on to finishing school in Switzerland and, as far as the Detective could ascertain, had remained in Switzerland and was not a part of the business.

When Pietre heard this he had been gutted. All this money being spent on finding out the whereabouts of Sylvia and they had reached another dead end! Maybe after talking to Sven Hendrickson about the "business deal" he could persuade him to at least let Sylvia know he had been asking after her.

A little over 24 hours later and a bewildered, elated and nervous Pietre was sitting in the back of his limousine trying to make sense of what exactly had happened.

Pietre had been shown into the board room and, politely, told to wait. After a few moments the door had opened and into the room stepped Sylvia! Pietre had stood there with his mouth open not quite knowing what to say. Sylvia had gasped and quickly sat down. The atmosphere had been electric between them Pietre was certain until he had looked into Sylvia's eyes and had seen her struggling to control the tears which were threatening to cascade down her beautiful face! Pietre had apologised for the deception and had volunteered to leave immediately but Sylvia had asked him to stay.

Sven Hendrickson had been troubled with a heart condition for many years and, unfortunately, his condition had deteriorated rapidly in recent months. Sylvia had persuaded the other Board Members that it was not in the Company's best interest if news of her Father's condition became public knowledge and she had pledged the Board Members that she would run the Company with their help until such time that a buyer could be discreetly found and the Company would pass into their hands on the passing of her Father. As she had told him this the tears had coursed down her beautiful cheeks and Pietre had held out his hand to gently brush them away. The effect on Sylvia had been startling to say the least. She had sprung up out of her chair and demanded that he leave the building immediately. She had shouted at him that he had been cruel in coming here under false pretences and she would not do business with him if he was the only person left in the world!

Pietre had been in a terrible quandary. He did not know what to do? He always knew what to do! Should he go and never look back just as Sylvia's father had done? Should he try and explain that all he had wanted to do was find her and ask what had gone so terribly wrong? As these thoughts struggled for supremacy Pietre knew exactly what he must do- and so he had walked around the large Conference table that separated him from his beloved Sylvia and held her tight as, at first, she had struggled to get out of his grasp and he had continued to hold her as the tears wracked her body. As the tears slowly subsided Sylvia had confessed that she had been devastated about her Father's reaction to meeting Pietre. She had never seen anyone quite as angry as her Father had been that night and she admitted that, for the first time in her life, she had been afraid, very afraid, of her Father.

Sylvia had called the other Members of the Board to a meeting that afternoon to discuss the outcome of the appointment with Mr Smith! She had attempted a feeble laugh when she had said Mr Smith- what the hell had he been thinking of when he called himself Mr Smith she had asked? He had had the good grace to blush at that as he sheepishly admitted that that idea was not one of his best! The stilted, awkward, laughter that followed had gone some way towards lightening the mood in the Conference room. Sylvia had telephoned her Secretary to cancel the scheduled meeting and she would get back to them in due course. Pietre had been both proud and impressed with the way Sylvia had collected her thoughts and the decisive way she had taken control of the bizarre situation she suddenly found herself in.

As the silence stretched out Pietre made another decision- one that he hoped with all his heart was the right one. He had told Sylvia that he had never stopped loving her and he told her that he was aghast at her Father's reaction at their one and only meeting.

He had held his breath like some love struck teenager as he studied Sylvia's face to see just what his outburst had meant to her.

Sylvia, meanwhile, had been surprised and absolutely delighted by Pieter's outburst but she was in a quandary. Whilst she had told Pieter a little about her Father's condition she had not told him the whole truth. Her Father was dying. Despite all the money at their disposal nothing could be done for him. They had told him to go home, rest, and enjoy what time he had left with his Family and under no circumstances was he to put himself under any undue stress! He had stepped down immediately but only on the strict understanding that Sylvia was to take control of the day to day running of the business. This had been some 3 months before and during that time Sylvia had had a baptism of fire! Almost all of the other Board Members had welcomed her with open arms and had voiced their intention of giving her every bit of help she felt she might need. Almost all of the Members! She had soon discovered a small number of them had smiled sweetly to her face but had been plotting to have her removed from the Board at the first opportunity! Sylvia had been staggered by the ferocity of the venom she had experienced. These people she had thought of as, whilst not quite friends, good loyal Board Members had tried to stab her in the back.

As she sat looking at her hands in the almost unbearable silence Pieter simply stood looking at her with a look of sheer terror on his face. What had he done? How stupid could one man be? He had surely frightened her away. He could not bear the silence any longer and so he slowly, with complete tenderness lifted her face until he could gaze into her eyes. His courage very nearly failed him but he forced himself to hold her gaze .He thought his heart would burst inside his body as he waited. Sylvia looked at him for a long moment and Pieter could see all sorts of emotions cross over her beautiful face. At long last she spoke" Pieter, please don't look at me like that. I really can't bear it." Pieter slowly dropped his hands and turned away. He so desperately wanted to declare his love and devotion for a second time but he did not have the courage and so he simply walked to the door, opened it and went dejectedly through it.

He sat in the limousine for several minutes in complete silence. The chauffeur he had hired asked him if he wanted to be taken back to the hotel but Pieter didn't hear a thing- he was too wrapped up in his own thoughts to register what the man had said. The chauffeur asked him once more what he wanted to do and Pieter told him resignedly that yes he would like to go back to the hotel. All the way there Pieter's thoughts kept going over the last few minutes. He was convinced that Sylvia still had some feelings for him but she had just let him walk out! What the hell was he supposed to do now?

Chapter 15.

Benjamin Smythson lay awake tenderly looking at his sleeping Wife. They had lived near Stockholm for several years now and he hoped and prayed that the beautiful Jessica was, finally, coming back to him. Oh! Not in a physical way but in a mental and emotional way. He had arranged for her to be seen by the finest Doctor's that he could afford and they had all said similar things. Time was a great healer, fresh air and stimuli of different sorts might help etc. At times Benjamin had begun to despair until that amazing, wonderful day just over a year ago. Looking back over that momentous year Benjamin could not believe the events that had happened. Jessica had told him that she was pregnant! Pregnant! That aspect of their marriage had always troubled him somewhat. His wife had never refused him anything regarding sex but he had always been troubled by the emotional distance she had maintained between them. Anyone meeting them or even knowing them would have never realised that anything was wrong. Jessica played the part of the hostess with great aplomb but Benjamin knew that the laughter and smiles she gave to their new friends and colleagues never came from her soul and he had doubted that they ever would. Until that fateful day! Jessica had seemed even more withdrawn than usual and in a burst of unheard of frustration Benjamin had lost his temper. Benjamin never lost his temper – ever!

As the tears had coursed down the cheeks of his adored Wife Benjamin had never felt more contrite in his abject apologies. He had begged for her forgiveness. He had shown such remorse that when he had looked upon Jessica's face he had been most perturbed to see a half smile playing at the corners of her luscious mouth. Just what was going on he had wondered to himself. Jessica had continued to smile enigmatically at him as she slowly, and gently, took hold of his hand and delicately placed it on her belly! For several long seconds Benjamin had not realised the significance of Jessica' actions until, suddenly and amazingly, the penny dropped! They were going to have a child. They were going to have a child! Benjamin remembered his reaction that day. He had leapt up as though he had had an electric shock and then he had whooped and hollered so much that Jessica had begged him to be quiet before someone wondered if he had lost his mind and would carry him off to the local asylum.

The pregnancy could not have gone better and with it had come a change in Jessica. She had blossomed both in body and mind at the prospect of Motherhood.

Albert Joseph Smythson was a healthy 8lbs 10ozs at birth. The delivery had been uneventful and both Mother and baby were doing fine. Jessica was a natural Mother and the bond between all three of them was truly delightful to see. There was only one cloud on the horizon though. What about the "gift". Would their son be blighted by it? Would it affect his life forever? They would not know for a while yet but Albert was now a few months old and appeared to be a "normal" baby. Jessica hoped with all her heart that Benjamin's genetics might be dominant in their son who bore an uncanny likeness to his Father. Could this help in "diluting the "Gift"?

As the years went on Jessica became less traumatised and troubled by the events that had happened so long ago in England. True, she would perhaps always be affected by them at certain times in her life but Jessica no longer saw as many dead people as she once did and she had grown very adept at ignoring them to such an extent that, eventually, most of them had given up trying to engage her in conversation – not least because most of them spoke Swedish! Jessica smiled to herself as she recalled this. Benjamin had set about learning the language immediately upon their arrival but Jessica's poor mental health had stopped her for attempting to learn for several months. Now, however, Jessica was fairly proficient in speaking and understanding Swedish – a fact that she was secretly proud of – but she was also grateful for the respite she had had from the constant voices and sightings!

The one, overriding, thing that she could never escape from was visualising the awful events of her wedding day.

Jessica Smythson had lay screaming on the Hall floor as guests tried desperately to save the lives of her Mother and Father. She was inconsolable in her grief. Benjamin Smythson, usually so calm in a crisis, was completely unable to stem the heart wrenching sound emanating from his bride. She had howled and howled as the lifeless bodies of both Joshua and Flora were taken away. She had refused to move since then. She sat cradling her blood stained bouquet as she rocked back and forth all through that long anguished night. Benjamin had not left her side for an instant. She could not quite believe what had happened.
She had looked on in disbelieving terror as events took their course. The sounds had been horrendous. The images would last on her mind forever but the most awful thing was that, somehow, the man had got away! He had seemed unnaturally strong as several brave guests struggled to pin him down. He had hurled one man across the room breaking his arm and he had stabbed another clean through the heart when that unfortunate man had stood in his way. It was all so unbelievable. In the awful chaos that followed nobody had been brave enough to tackle the man again and he had simply walked through the door and out into the night!

Would she ever know what had become of that dreadful man?

Arthur Stump had walked, almost casually, away from the carnage he had left behind at the wedding reception. He had held the gaze of everyone who had had the audacity to look him in the eye! He did not know their names but he would recognise every single one of them in an instant. He would not hesitate to kill them all. He was invincible. He was a direct descendant of the inimitable Lizzie Stump! As the name of Lizzie came, uninvited, into his head Arthur's demeanour changed. Do not think about Lizzie! Do not think about Lizzie!

Lizzie Stump, meanwhile, had no such qualms about invading the mind of Arthur. Oh! He had done quite well in killing both Joshua and Flora but what about Jessica? Jessica must die if true revenge was to be exacted on the family who had destroyed her own. Arthur Stump was naïve in the extreme if he thought his troubles were over.

That night was the most torturous night of Arthur's miserable existence. Every time he closed his eyes he could see Lizzie hovering by his bed whispering to him about what he needed to do next.

Eventually Arthur could bear it no longer and sat on the edge of the bed pleading for it to stop. He would do anything for it to stop. Anything! Arthur's heart almost burst out of his scrawny body as suddenly, and completely terrifyingly, Lizzie Stump was standing right in front of him telling him exactly what he must do. Lizzie was dead! He had cradled her lifeless body with his own arms. He had seen the life drain away from her. What the hell was going on?

A few minutes later and the final vestige of decency and sanity had left the pathetic body of Arthur Stump to be replaced by the malevolent presence of the evil Lizzie Stump.

Lizzie's plan was to be implemented immediately and all Arthur had to do was to go to the hovel he called home- collect his daughter and what few miserable possessions they had and leave Saham Toney never to return. Arthur sensed in the darkest recesses of his fevered mind that he was unlikely to escape from Lizzie but he was too exhausted and weak willed to challenge her any more.

The next morning and Arthur was in position just the other side of the garden wall where less than 24hours earlier the terrible ordeal of the wedding massacre was still evident. There were more people around than he had anticipated and he had almost cried out when he had heard Benjamin Smythson organising a manhunt for him. Benjamin had offered a reward of 20 guineas to the man who brought Arthur to him. He also offered a further 10 guineas if Arthur were still alive. How the hell had he gotten himself into such a situation? Arthur knew the answer to that. Lizzie Stump - his Aunt. It had taken all of Arthur's willpower, or should that be Lizzie's willpower, not to turn and run for his life without doing what he had come here to do. Arthur knew that he would never be left in peace and so he waited, patiently, for the right moment to present itself.

After more than 6 hours of squatting in a tree Arthur's patience was rewarded. Jessica was being led outside by a servant. Jessica was still sobbing hysterically as the servant was trying to help her to the outside facilities. Jessica could barely walk and the anguish on her face made Arthur look away. He had done that to her! He had done that! No Aunt Lizzie had done that- not him. Suddenly the sound in his head became unbearable as Lizzie's voice shrieked at him. The sound that came from within his head was a sound he had never heard before. It was a deep, guttural, primeval sound that started really low in the centre of his brain and slowly and inexorably began to rise in both volume and pitch until Arthur could bear it no longer. With an inhuman screech Arthur Stump launched himself out of his hiding place and ran blindly at Jessica Smythson.

Arthur never knew what killed him. All he knew was that the sounds in his head stopped instantaneously. Then slowly, and utterly unbelievably, he was standing by the side of his own body. At least he thought it was his own body. It was hard to tell as most of the right side of his face had disappeared!

The next day Arthur's human form, if you could describe Arthur Stump as human, was hauled into the village square where all the villagers had gathered to see the spectacle of the remains of the man who had killed all those people on what should have been a joyous occasion. Arthur's other body stood a little apart from Lizzie Stump.

Lizzie was in a very agitated frame of mind and Arthur had steered clear of her. Arthur's heart skipped a beat as he saw someone in the crowd. His Daughter! No-one in the village knew about his Daughter. Arthur Stump had made sure about that. Her Mother had died in childbirth and they had been forced to flee their home when rumours of witchcraft began to circulate.

Arthur knew that Mary shared his "gift" but he was absolutely astounded when Lizzie walked straight up to her and began talking! Arthur knew that Mary could hear Lizzie and Arthur thought his heart might stop-again- when Lizzie pointed to Arthur across the village green and Mary looked straight at him!

Suddenly the crowd surged forward and Arthur could not believe what he was seeing. His earthly body was being lifted onto a bonfire and being burnt! How could they do this to him! He was innocent! Lizzie Stump was the guilty one. At the thought of Lizzie Arthur looked around desperately trying to catch sight of her. Out of the corner of his eye he spotted Mary standing quite alone away from the crowds but just as Arthur got close Mary just nodded almost imperceptibly and walked away. The look of triumph on Lizzie's face was the last conscious thought as the most incredible pain he had every suffered wracked his body. No-one but Lizzie heard his screams as both his human form and his "ghostly" form began to smoulder and burn. It took Arthur Stump over 2 hours to die. Lizzie Stump sat patiently at his side never once looking in his direction and never once telling him just what exactly she had said to Mary.

Maybe now it was all over thought Arthur as he slipped into oblivion. Maybe or maybe not!

Chapter 16.

Sylvia sat impassively in the Boardroom. Her mind was a maelstrom of conflicting emotions. She had been both alarmed and delighted to see Pietre - but she now did not know what to do! She adored her Father but, despite herself, she still loved Pietre with an ache she had tried to suppress all these months. The instant she saw him she knew that she would always love Pietre Mortenson but what should she do? Her beloved Father was dying, she was losing her battle to stay on the Board, and she did not know what to do!!

A little over an hour later and Sylvia left the office for the day with strict instructions to her trusted Secretary to inform her immediately if there was anything untoward happening with some of the more dangerous members of the Company. Elizabeth had simply looked Sylvia in the eye and nodded almost imperceptibly. Elizabeth was only too aware of the machinations going on around her. She might only be a lowly Secretary but Elizabeth possessed an enviable quality. She would remain completely loyal to the Company. If she could help in any small way then she was going to do just that. Over the years working for the Company she had amassed enough delicate information about key members of the Board and their little peccadillos and foibles and she knew that she would have no compunction in revealing her information to Sylvia when the time was right. With a satisfied smile playing softly at the corners of her mouth Elizabeth set to work!

As Sylvia quietly opened the imposing door of the family home her courage almost failed her. What she was about to do could go horribly wrong. What she was about to do could kill her beloved Father but she knew, deep down, that she had no choice and so she gently opened the door to her Father's suite of rooms and went in.

Sven Hendrickson stirred from his light sleep as he sensed someone coming into the room. Not more Doctors or Nurses please! He had had enough of them all. He just needed to rest a while longer and he would be fit enough to go back to work and continue being a force to be reckoned with. As he opened his eyes he smiled. It was not the medics but his beautiful only child. As his eyes focussed Sven became concerned. He had never seen the expression on his Daughter's face before. She looked both frightened and determined in equal measure. Slowly he raised himself up and faced his Daughter.

Sylvia sat quietly holding her Father's hand as he struggled to contain his emotions. Sven could not look at her. Sylvia waited. Slowly, inexorably, the truth came out. Sven admitted that he had been alarmed and traumatised when he had seen Pietre. His mind had gone back all those years to a time when he had loved Pieter's mother and she had loved him! Sven told Sylvia everything. He told her about the love affair he had had. He told her that he had always wondered if he was the Father of Pietre and not Bernhard. He told her of his horror at the prospect of his beautiful Daughter having a relationship with someone who might turn out to be her half-brother! Sylvia had recoiled in terror as the awful truth hit her. She had slept with Pietre! She had slept with her own half-brother! Oh my God! What should she do now?

He had cried so much that Sylvia worried that all of this misery might prove to be too much for her beloved Father but as Sven had gently told her – he was made of strong stuff.

He also told her he knew just how little time he had left! Sylvia had tried to cajole him at first but Sven had gripped her hand in a feverish way and told her to be quiet until he had finished speaking. Sylvia had done just that and was amazed by what she had been told. All those years her Father had worshipped another man's wife! All those years the hatred between him and Bernhard had continued. So that was why the animosity had started. Sven admitted that he had loved two women at the same time. How was that possible? Sylvia had always thought her Parent's had been blissfully happy and Sven had assured her that they had been. Your Mother was the most amazing woman her Father had said. She had known about the affair from the very beginning and had chosen her own path. She knew that Sven adored her and would never leave her but she also realised that the love her husband had for this other woman was just as strong. At the thought of her Mother Sylvia smiled. She had been a beautiful woman but her inner beauty had always shone through. Everyone who had ever met her had fallen under her spell!

Sylvia and Sven spent the rest of the day together. At the end of the afternoon Sylvia knew what she needed to do. She needed to speak to Pietre and tell him the truth! How she would go about it she had no idea but Pietre Mortennson needed to know. As she waited for the hotel receptionist to put her through to Pieter's room Sylvia thought her heart would break.

When Pietre heard Sylvia's voice his legs almost buckled underneath him. What did she want?

Moments later and Pietre was heading down to the offices of the Hendrickson Corporation once again. As he entered the building he was surprised to see Sylvia's secretary waiting for him and he was immediately ushered into an elevator he had not noticed before and seconds later he was sitting in the sumptuous surroundings of Sven Hendrickson's private quarters where a nervous Sylvia was waiting with a large Scotch for them both!

Pietre sat in shock as the realisation of what he had just been told began to sink in. Sylvia couldn't be his half-sister surely? Dear God! They had slept together! The enormity of the situation had, at first, threatened to overwhelm them both. They had talked into the small hours and Pietre had accepted Sylvia's invitation to stay the night in the Guest Suite as it was very late.

Sleep had eluded both of them and so as dawn broke they were both in the kitchen drinking coffee and staring into the distance. Pietre began to speak at exactly the same second as Sylvia and the forced bonhomie between them had been excruciating. They had always been able to speak openly when they were together but this was horrendous. Pietre apologised and said that Sylvia should go ahead and speak first.

As Sylvia began to outline her proposal Pietre began to smile. Sylvia wanted him to have a D.N.A test to confirm if he was indeed her half-brother but that was not what was making him smile. No! What was making him smile was the simple act of Sylvia gently holding his hand and telling him that she hoped with all her heart that Pietre was not her half-brother but was someone she could continue to love again!

Pietre had never fully appreciated the power that being wealthy could give you. Just a few phone calls later and they were heading for a private hospital to have the test done! He had been assured of the absolute discretion of the Clinic. Elizabeth, Sylvia's amazing Secretary, had arranged it for him without any qualms. She was invaluable Sylvia had admitted during their amazing reconciliation. They had both never stopped talking for the last few hours. Pietre sensed that the non-stop conversation was a distraction technique. He knew just how nervous and appalled they both felt at the prospect of the wrong result but they had stoically refused to speak about it. What they would do if the worst happened neither of them could countenance right now. They would have to deal with it at some point but not right now!

As they waited in the lounge for the appointment time to slowly come around Sylvia had been absolutely honest about the battles she had faced on her own whilst her Father had been so ill. Pietre thought his heart would break as he saw the anguish in her eyes and so he had simply held her hands and listened.

As he listened an idea began to formulate in his mind. An idea so outlandish that he wondered where it had come from. He knew that he could not do anything about it right now but when this current nightmare was over he had some telephone calls to make.

Chapter 17.

Harold Carrington replaced the telephone receiver and stood looking at the phone for a moment or two. He had been surprised to hear Pieter's voice on the other end. He had been even more surprised at Pieter's request. Harold had always prided himself on his ability to "read" people. His pride was feeling a little dented right now as he realised that he was nowhere near as adept at "reading" people as he had presumed.

"Maud! Where are you? I have some news for you!" Harold allowed the merest hint of a smile to hover at the corners of his mouth. He hardly ever answered the telephone. He always assumed that anyone telephoning would want to speak to the redoubtable Maud and he was rarely incorrect, but how wrong was he right now?

Maud Carrington smiled inwardly to herself as she sat, impassively, listening to her beloved Harold as he outlined Pieter's plan to her. "What good is all his wealth doing him anyway?" Harold had asked rather pointedly to Maud. Harold and Maud had always been financially astute and had both benefitted from having wealthy Parent's and Grandparent's. Harold continued to pace up and down the kitchen at "Haven's Retreat" as he formulated his part in Pieter's scheme.

Maud busied herself with making preparations for her Daughter and her family on their return. The kitchen was the place that every gravitated to during times of excitement, trepidation or downright fear pondered Maud. This house was so beautiful and so full of character mused Maud as she carefully arranged the dining table ready for that evening's meal. As Maud crossed the downstairs landing she was suddenly and frighteningly aware of an incredible sense of foreboding! As she looked nervously around her Maud was shocked to see that she was shaking – violently. What was happening? Why did she feel like this? Maud Carrington spoke harshly to her inner self and chided herself for being a silly old woman. Pull yourself together old girl! Just at that moment she heard a car arriving on the gravel driveway and so all silly thoughts were put to the back of her mind as she raced to open the front door and she her family once more. She had so many questions to ask them about their trip!

Elijah Stump sat high up in a large tree surveying the grounds surrounding "Haven's Retreat". He looked and felt terrible. He had not been seen by anyone in the village for weeks and he was aware that people must be talking. He had avoided all contact with his Parent's but he was certain that they did not know of his whereabouts and Elijah was grateful that his Parent's had not done anything about trying to ascertain them. From an early age Elijah had done his own thing, he had disappeared for the day on many occasions as a small boy and for even longer as he had aged. His Parent's had finally given up trying to tie him down and over the years his relationship with them both had collapsed totally. They seemed to neither know nor care where the hell he was and right now that suited Elijah Stump just fine! Lizzie's voice interrupted his contemplation. Would that bloody woman ever give him peace?

As Maud was getting ready for bed later that night she smiled as she remembered the expressions on the faces of her delightful Grandchildren as they had tripped over each other's words in their eagerness to explain just what a fantastic holiday they had all had. She also remembered them saying just how lovely it was to get back to "Haven's Retreat" and its serene calmness after the hectic schedule they had endured. Maud did not feel serene or calm – in fact she felt very strange indeed. Twice during the evening as she had crossed the downstairs landing she had had the same sense of foreboding and doom. What was going on in the house? Oh! She realised that a house of this age would have a history but she had never suspected that the house would have had such a perturbing feel about it after all this time that her Daughter and family had lived here. Maybe she should ask Elspeth about it? Or maybe, you foolish old woman, you should just go to bed – right now!

As sleep finally began to overtake her Maud decided that, if she had the courage and if she could risk the obvious questions about senility and the state of her mental health she WOULD ask Elspeth about the house. Wouldn't she?

The next morning dawned bright and sunny and Maud, once again, dismissed her silly thoughts from the previous day. You silly old fool thought Maud as she began to clear away the breakfast dishes as she listened to the excited chatter of her Grandchildren.

Elsewhere in the house different emotions were in play as Gerry entered the office to look at any e-mails that needed his attention before he went back to the Surgery the next day. As he crossed the landing to go into his office he stopped dead. He had never really taken to the space that now contained his office but he was an intelligent, rational man who was being completely ridiculous! Gerry Carrington squared his shoulders and unlocked the room and went in.

30 minutes later and Gerry admitted defeat. That room had got the better of him for the first, and hopefully, the last time. Most of the time Gerry had spent in that room had been spent on trying to find ways to convince Elspeth that it would be a good idea to use one of the barns outside as his new office. It would have more space. It would not encroach on the house any more (he had serious doubts about that angle as his office did not encroach on the house at all). He could convert the barns to enable the children to have their own spaces and that would allow Elspeth to work her design magic on his office space. That might work eh?

As Gerry was about to enter the kitchen he heard Elspeth let out a surprised giggle and then issue an abject apology to his Mother-in-law who stormed out of the kitchen looking less than pleased.

After Elspeth had finished telling him about her Mother's deranged feelings about the landing Gerry decided that now was not the time to talk to Elspeth about his own fears. Now was the time to speak to Maud!

Chapter 18.

Harold was pleased with himself – very pleased in fact. He had risen early that morning with a sense of purpose and resolve he had not felt for a very long time. Pietre had entrusted him with a very delicate task. He had asked him to look into the possibility of purchasing shares in the Hendrickson Corporation on his behalf. He had explained, briefly, some of the reasons for his wanting acquisition of the shares but Harold knew that Pietre was holding something back. He also knew that he would enjoy the challenge set for him and so he had started his day by telephoning Sweden. What had changed in his life so much that he, Harold Carrington Retired general, was telephoning Sylvia's secretary for inside information regarding the hostile takeover of the Hendrickson Corporation he had absolutely no idea, but what he did know was that he was going to give it his best shot for the sake of Pieter and his bride to be. He had grown extremely fond of the Swedish man and so he listened as Elizabeth gave him some of the information he needed. It would take some time to acquire enough shares discreetly to enable Pietre to have a controlling interest in the Hendrickson Corporation. What had clinched it for Harold was the analogy that the Hendrickson board members were Pieter's enemy and, as a highly decorated ex member of her Majesty's army, Pietre knew that he would be up to the job. Pietre had asked him to try to complete the purchase of the stocks and shares within the month, if possible, and to keep him informed as and when he could. "All very hush hush mind Harold" Pietre had whispered to him. Harold had agreed instantly. Now, however, his nerves threatened to get the better of him. He was not a high flying business man. He did not know the first thing about business and yet Pietre had entrusted him with the task and, by Jove, he would not let him down.

Harold had been absolutely staggered at the amount of money Pietre had put into the new account solely for the purpose of acquiring shares. It was an astronomical amount of money! Harold had not appreciated just how wealthy young Pietre really was! Harold's thoughts were interrupted by the sound of Elizabeth wishing him a" very good morning" and" was he ready for the first day's work" He was ready – he was more than ready.

Elijah Stump lay in the makeshift bed in a quiet cove deep within the woods. Anyone passing outside would have been horrified at the wailing noises emanating from the barn- they did not sound human. He was still alive! The voice in his head was still there. He had not had the courage to kill himself after all. He was a complete failure! Elijah remembered, with a shudder, the first time he had thought that. The voice inside his head had been deafening in its condemnation of his attempt to kill himself. Did he not know how important he was? Did he not realise that he MUST do what she demanded of him? He must kill the blonde stranger if he wanted any sort of respite from his torture. If the blonde stranger was killed then the voice promised him she would finally leave him in peace. The prospect of peace for Elijah was what ultimately convinced him to do what the voice told he must do. Peace! How Elijah needed peace right now. In his infrequent lucid moments Elijah knew his mind was jumping back and forth regarding the events of the last few months. Had he killed that woman in the pub? Had he imagined killing her or had he, in fact, done it? He couldn't remember. He couldn't remember much with any degree of certainty any more. What was he to do? The voice told him again that the blonde stranger had killed his relation Lizzie.

Elijah began to shake uncontrollably as his thoughts returned to what little he knew about Lizzie Stump. He remembered, vaguely, his Grandparents whispering in fear and dread about the infamous Lizzie and how she had brought shame on the Stump name.

How she had "spoken" to his unfortunate ancestor all those years ago. Elijah felt an immense sympathy for his distant relation. How he must have suffered at the hands of Lizzie.

As the dawn came up in all its glory Elijah was a beaten man. He knew what he MUST do. He was so tired, so very tired, and he was not strong enough to fight any more. If he killed the blonde stranger then he might be at peace. With a supreme effort Elijah Stump climbed out of bed and looked at his surroundings. How had his life come to this? How had he allowed himself to become so distant from reality? All Elijah knew was that he had had enough and if it took the death of this stranger – then so be it!

Chapter 19.

Gerry Carrington was a confident, successful Plastic Surgeon whose patients were a little in awe and not a little in love with him! So why was he dithering outside his Mother-in –law's bedroom like a nervous schoolboy outside the Headmaster's study? Gerry took a deep breath and knocked on the door. When Maud answered he could tell immediately that something was wrong. Maud looked terrible. She was shaking and she looked as though she had been crying. Gerry's courage almost failed him- almost but not quite- and he looked Maud straight in the eye and began speaking.

A little over half an hour later and both of them stood silently looking at each other. They had always had a good relationship with each other but, suddenly, they could not look each other in the eye. Gerry finally broke the awkward silence. "Maud, I know that this all seems too ridiculous for words but we both know that something is going on in this house don't we? I have tried to be rational about this and I can't. I have one other confession to make. I think Gordon Jarvis knows more than he is letting on. Do you remember the last time we were all in this room together? And Gordon couldn't get out of the office fast enough? What if he does know something and he isn't telling us? What then eh? Maud listened to her son-in-law and knew he was right. Maybe it was time to talk to Gordon about the house and what went on last year when he had stayed as a guest of the previous owners.

Did they both have the courage to ask him outright what he knew? There was only one way to find out. With that determined look on her face that stopped grown men in their tracks Maud Carrington collected her handbag and coat and strode purposefully towards the front door with Gerry trailing behind her.

The moment Gordon saw the expression on the faces of the two people standing at the bar in front of him he knew. He knew with absolute certainty what they had come to talk to him about and he felt sick. He felt sick to the pit of his stomach but he also knew that now was the time for the truth to be told. He could not, and would not, put it off any longer and so he ushered his new found friends upstairs to the pub's private quarters and told Mavis that she should come upstairs as soon as she could.

Mavis Riley – the indefatigable landlady of the local hostelry – was nervous. Very nervous. She was aware of some of the events that had happened the previous summer, but not all of them, and when she had seen the haunted expression on her beloved Gordon's face she had been taken aback. What the hell was wrong? Why was Gordon taking Maud and Gerry upstairs? As soon as she was able to Maud joined her Husband and her friends.

As she entered her lounge the silence was palpable. Gordon sat by the fire staring into space and both Maud and Gerry looked aghast. Gordon had told them about the tragic events of the previous summer and he had confessed that he had used this as an excuse for not returning to the farmhouse. But this had been a lie. He also admitted that he found the farmhouse office a terrible place to be in.

"Whenever I go in there it's as if I can't breathe. I have this terrible feeling of something evil in that room. I know that sounds ridiculous, but it's the truth." shuddered Gordon as he studiously avoided any eye contact. Mavis's heart went out to her beloved. She knew how hard it must have been to say that out loud. In the short time they had been together Mavis knew that Gordon prided himself on being a "man's man" who had no truck with fanciful notions. He called a spade a spade and respected anyone who did the same.

It was decided, much later that night, after they had spoken together that it was imperative that they all speak to Pietre together. Gordon had reluctantly admitted that he shared Gerry's view that Pietre also had the same feelings about that room. "When Pietre returns from Sweden we will talk to him then" Gerry had said quietly and forcefully. No-one in the room made any objections and so it was that they all said goodnight and wished each other a peaceful night's sleep! They all knew that sleep would be impossible but in the stalwart tradition of the English everyone ignored the irony of the situation!

Harold wondered where the hell Maud had got to. Elspeth had told him, eventually, about how she had laughed at the ridiculous suggestion by her Mother that maybe the house was haunted!

Harold did not think for a second that the house was haunted. Stuff and nonsense he had always said. People's vivid imagination was to blame. Only ignorant, ill-educated people believe in such tosh! So why was he pacing around downstairs waiting impatiently for his Wife and Son-in-law to return? Why could he not shake of this strange feeling that they may be right after all? When Maud did, eventually, return he would speak to her and have it out once and for all. It was beyond ridiculous. Wasn't it?

Chapter 20.

The events of the last few days had been exceptional! Pietre had returned from Sweden and had admitted that he too felt the same about the house. They had all agreed that they needed to find out as much about the house as they possibly could. Oscar Washington had been contacted and he had promised to do as much as he possibly could to ascertain the origins of the house. He had admitted to carrying out a little research off his own bat and he hoped that they would not mind too much!

Oscar believed that the house had been built in 1732 by a family called the Bromfield's. They appeared on the relevant Census and so he was as certain as he could be that this information was correct. Pietre had made contact with the Agency in Sweden who, unbeknown to anyone, had discovered that Pietre was almost certainly related to the Bromfield's as Swedish records showed that a family from England had settled there at about the right time. It was not guaranteed of course but the names and dates did appear to match.

Pietre knew in his heart that his search for his ancestors began and ended here at "Haven's Retreat". How he knew he could not quantify – he just KNEW!

All the local records seemed to confirm this. One thing, however, could not be confirmed. And that was- why was there a Wedding Certificate and a Death Certificate issued on the same day when Church records did not show that a burial had taken place? How could that be?

The Reverend Wellbeloved had done some more research regarding this but had drawn a blank – except for an old wives tale about a feud between 2 families that was still talked about in certain circles within the village to this day!

The very second Pietre heard the Reverend Wellbeloved say the name Lizzie Stump he immediately sensed that this was really important. He did not KNOW it was important but he sensed it with every fibre of both his body and his mind.

Angela Barnes stood quietly and timidly in the hallway of "Haven's Retreat" and waited patiently. She had lived her entire life here in the village of Saham Toney and not once had she set foot in the grounds of the house let alone inside the house itself! Just wait until she got back home and told them all about it! She had been the cleaner at the Vicarage for years and her Mother and Grandmother before her. There had been a member of the Stanier family associated with the village for over 300 years and Angela prided herself on her family's intimate knowledge of the people of Saham Toney. Not that she was a gossip mind! Oh No. She was the soul of discretion. Didn't she know many things about the village and its history? Didn't she know things about the people in the village that maybe she shouldn't? But she was not one to idly gossip and spread rumours. Was she?

Sometime later, when Angela Barnes had left, everyone around the kitchen table sat in quiet reflection regarding what they had all heard. Angela told them that the Stanier's and the Stump's had always lived together in the village for as long as anyone knew. What everyone in the village also knew was that there was no love lost between both families.

They had always kept their distance from each other and it was an unspoken family law that they would NEVER speak to each other or have any contact whatsoever. Angela had never understood exactly why and no-one in her family could tell her why either. It was just something that had to be obeyed, Angela Barnes took great delight in telling the assembled people around the rather beautiful table in the gorgeous kitchen of this beautiful house that the Stumps were ostracised by most of the villagers and had been for generations because everyone KNEW that they were all witches didn't they? Oh she realised that sophisticated people like you did not believe in such things but, believe me, it was true Angela had declared. It had never been proven of course but that did not mean it was not true Angela had said as she was ushered out of the hallway and through the front door.

Oh! What things she would be able to tell all of her friends – and some of her enemies-thought Angela as she took one last, lingering, look at "Haven's Retreat."

Little did Angela realise just what she had unleashed on the village and the occupants of the cottage she had just left.

Lizzie Stump was incandescent with pure, unadulterated hatred! How dare that snivelling Angela spread malicious gossip about her family? How dare she?

Lizzie's voice went quiet in the head of Elijah as he stood silently in the background listening to Angela holding court. When Lizzie went quiet Elijah was more worried than ever. For the last week Lizzie had plagued him day and night. She had never shut up! She never let up for a second and Elijah wondered just how much more of this he could take – but the quiet was even more terrifying!!

"Oh! I know I shouldn't say anything really, but EVERYONE knows about the Stump's don't they? They have always been outsiders haven't they? And as for that weasel Elijah, well, you only have to take one look at him to realise that he isn't right in the head. Don't you eh?"

Suddenly Angela became aware of a change in the atmosphere around her. Everybody began to disperse and look extremely uncomfortable. Seconds later and there was a voice whispering softly in her ear? It was a voice that she had never heard before but Angela Barnes nee Stanier felt her blood chill in her veins. She knew with terrible certainty just who was speaking to her. Lizzie Stump! Oh my God! Even as she slowly turned towards Elijah she sensed what was about to happen. What she did not realise was how sudden and horrific her death would be!

The scene of crime that presented itself to the Police and Forensics evidence looked more like something from a horror movie. Angela's body lay where she had fallen. Police Constable James Whittaker did not have to take a second look as he escorted the detectives to the scene. He would never forget the look on the victim's face – or rather – what remained of her face! Elijah Stump had stabbed Angela in the throat and had attempted to cut her tongue out. Attempted but not quite succeeded. Angela looked as though she was trying to scream as she had died. The lower part of her face had been almost completely severed.

The nightmarish rictus grin would give the young Constable nightmares for years. How could someone do something like this? And in front of dozens of witnesses! As Detective Youlgreave began to speak James forced himself to listen. Youlgreave was asking him, once again, how was it that Elijah Stump had managed to escape? Didn't anyone try and stop him? (Would you have tried to stop a psychopath with a large knife thought James?)

It had been established that Elijah Stump had disappeared into the night and had not been seen since. Where the hell had he gone? Detective Youlgreave was confident that he was still somewhere in the village as the roads out of the village had been blocked as soon as was possible. No reported sightings of the distinctive Elijah had been reported. So where the hell was the little toe-rag? Detective Youlgreave was, secretly, very pleased that the suspect had not been found. When he himself found and convicted Elijah Stump he would earn extra brownie points towards his inevitable promotion surely? He just need to be found – and quickly!

Mavis handed Gordon a stiff drink the second he had finished being questioned. Mavis had lived most of her adult life here at the pub but, right now, she did not have any desire to go into that bar ever again. The Police had told her that the pub would be closed for the foreseeable future as it was a crime scene. They had also told her that it would take a specialist team of cleaners to service the bar before they re-opened. Mavis doubted if she would ever re-open. She could not get the image of the carnage she had witnessed out of her mind. All that blood! All that blood from one poor unfortunate soul. Her thoughts were interrupted by Gordon speaking. "Mavis, my love, I need to go to "Haven's Retreat". I need to go NOW.

Elijah Stump sat, impassively looking at the front door of "Haven's Retreat". He had sat perfectly still for several hours waiting for the right moment to strike. Lizzie's voice insisted the he strike now but he had other ideas. Lizzie's voice became even shriller as she screamed at him to do as she ordered. Elijah ignored her. He was past caring any more. All he did know was that once he had killed the blond stranger he would be free. He would be free of the voices inside his head; he would be free from the mental torture he had endured for what seemed like forever. Elijah had decided that he would kill the stranger and then kill himself. What had he got to live for? As he thought this the sound of a vehicle arriving at the farmhouse brought his conscious thoughts to the forefront.

Mavis and Gordon had not spoken a single word to each other during the short car ride to the farmhouse. Neither had known quite what to say but they both realised, separately, that no words were actually necessary. They loved and respected each other totally and both knew that, somehow, they would both survive this and come out of this horrific tragedy intact as a couple, but right now they needed to get this next thing out of the way. Gordon had absolutely no idea just exactly what he was going to say all he did know was that this needed to be sorted- and sorted this very night!

Elijah could not believe his luck! Oh he knew that the place was surrounded by Police. He knew that this would be an almost impossible thing to do. Almost impossible-but not totally impossible.

Pietre opened the door and held his breath. The Police had been in touch with him to tell all the people here at the farmhouse the terrible thing that had happened in the bar that fateful afternoon.

It appeared that Elijah had been seen loitering around the village talking to himself even more then he usually did. He had been seen arguing with an unseen person in the high street and in the local park. Some of the witnesses to the atrocity had told the Police about the legend of the feud between the Stump' and the Stanier's. At first the Police had dismissed this as nothing more than an old wives tale, but as more and more people began telling them similar things it was decided to take the idea of a vendetta a little more seriously. It had been decided, after speaking to Gordon Jarvis, that a Police presence might be required at the farmhouse until this nutcase had been brought to justice!

Chapter 21.

The sound of dogs. The sound of dogs heading this way! Elijah hated dogs – hated them with a passion- especially Police dogs. He had to get away. He had to get away now. Lizzie would just have to wait a little longer for her revenge wouldn't she? Could he survive a moment longer with Lizzie's voice in his head? He did not know. What he did know was that now was not the time to kill the blonde stranger. He would never get near enough to him. He had only one chance at this – and now was not the right time. He could bide his time a little longer and plan it to perfection. Once it was done Elijah would be free.

Elijah crept down from his vantage point and, slowly and carefully, made his way back to the wood where he had been hiding since he had murdered that stupid woman who was talking about his family as though they were some sort of lunatics! How dare she have said that? How dare she? As he remembered some of the events that had happened Elijah began to giggle. She couldn't say anything now could she? She couldn't say anything without her tongue could she? The giggling got louder and louder and it took all of Elijah's diminished resolve not to run straight into the local high street and tell the world just exactly what he had done. They would take notice of him then wouldn't they? They would know just what they were dealing with wouldn't they? Suddenly Elijah realised that he could still hear the sounds of dogs – and they seemed to be getting louder and nearer! What the hell? He needed to throw them off his trail. Had they somehow got his scent? How the hell had that happened? Elijah wondered if the bastard Police had got to the hovel he called home and, somehow, gotten hold of something that held his scent. Could they do that? Could tracker dogs sniff him out? What the f*** was he to do now? Elijah began to run as a plan or sorts began to struggle to formulate in his addled brain. It might just work. It needed to work!

Elijah had heard the sound of the Police helicopter almost immediately after the events in the pub. How quickly had that helicopter got there? Was all this for him? Elijah had smiled to himself at that thought. All this for him? How important was he now eh? Who else in his family had had a Police helicopter looking for them? He was somebody now – wasn't he? Lizzie Stump I bet you didn't have a helicopter looking for you eh – did you? At this thought Elijah began to giggle uncontrollably. Of course she wouldn't have had. They didn't have them then did they? Did they? As the last vestiges of sanity and rational thought disappeared Elijah's survival instincts kicked back in once more. He knew what he must do. They would never find him if he could only get back to his hiding place. He was certain that the Police would never find him there. He just needed a little time that was all.

Elijah lay quietly as the sound of the dogs got closer and closer. He could barely breathe, the smell was so awful, but if he could just hold out a little bit longer then he was certain that he would be safe.

Elijah lay squashed into a deserted badger's sett that he had discovered during one of his late night explorations. For once he was glad that the stupid Government had arranged for a badger cull the previous year. How else would he be able to hide eh?

He had covered himself with fox faeces and the rotting remains of some birds he had found a few days before. He had just about managed to cover his tracks when he sensed the presence of a dog! The bloody animal was only inches from his face! What the hell would he do now if he was discovered? The Police dog was inching nearer and nearer when Elijah heard a voice less than 20 feet away from him! "Come away! Come away now- you stupid animal! It's just a badger sett. God! The stench of it. Bloody Hell! It reeks. Sarge? There's nothing here Sarge. Shall we move on to the next bit eh?" Elijah didn't quite hear what the reply was but waited hardly daring to breathe. Suddenly the sound of the dog and his handler began to fade. They were going. They were going away!

Elijah Stump lay in his hell hole for the rest of the day and all of that evening. He was taking no chances. He was taking no chances whatsoever. If the Police had searched this place thoroughly, as he thought they would think they had, then they would not be likely to return any time soon! Stupid f****** Police.

He had been given another chance. He would not let Lizzie down this time. Oh no! Lizzie's voice would finally be silenced – and not before time thought Elijah as sleep finally took over. Just wait for what the future would bring.

Chapter 22.

Pietre was staring unseeingly into the dying embers of the log fire at "Haven's Retreat" as Harold quietly closed the door to the lounge behind him and went to stand by the man who had become such a dear friend to him these last few weeks. It took several seconds for Pieter to realise that Harold was standing beside him and he looked startled when Harold spoke. "Sorry old chap- didn't mean to scare you. Are you okay? What a stupid bloody question. Of course you're not okay. How idiotic of me." Pietre shook his head to disengage his thoughts and turned to Harold. "I'm fine thanks – just a little overwhelmed by it all- that's all. How are you? How are the acquisitions proceeding eh?"

As he climbed the stairs at God knew what time Pietre began to feel a lot happier with the business side of things that he had thought possible. Harold and Elizabeth in Sweden had done an amazing job in persuading many of the existing shareholders to sell some of their shares to Harold's new Company. Harold, Elizabeth and Pietre all had the same feeling that the new Board members were not to be trusted with the handling of the future of the Hendrickson Corporation. He had been in constant touch with Sylvia about the state of her Father's health as well as the state of the takeover bid. Sylvia's father was deteriorating quickly and Pietre hoped the old man would live long enough to realise that his beloved Daughter was back in total charge of the family business. As he thought of Sylvia his heart skipped a beat. He loved her. He loved her so much. There was just one thing that had been stopping his happiness from being complete. The D.N.A test results. He had asked the Company to telephone him the instant that the results came through and they had telephoned him that very morning.

He was NOT the son of Hendrickson after all! He was his Father's son. He was his Father's son!!!

When he had heard this news Pieter had sobbed. He had sobbed uncontrollably for, possibly, the first time in his life. He had startled Elspeth and her family as the sound of his apparent anguish had reverberated around the entire house – or so it had seemed that morning as the entire Carrington household had been outside his bedroom door asking if he was okay? Pietre had spent an awkward few moments composing himself under the worried scrutiny of the lovely people in front of him. He had been genuinely moved by the concern of them all and so, with only a little persuasion from the redoubtable Maud, he had confessed his love for Sylvia Hendrickson. The smiles of the faces of his new friends brought a massive grin to his own face and, so it was, that he was almost dragged down the stairs – plonked onto one of the kitchen chairs – and told to spill! Spill? What do you mean Grace? Grace had given him one of her famous withering looks and said that if he didn't tell her and everyone else just when he was going to propose to the awesome Sylvia then she might just take it upon herself to ring Sweden and do it for him!

As this thought entered his head it went some way to dispelling his negative thoughts about the house – some way but not all the way. Just what had gone on in this house all those years ago? Just what was the connection with the Stump's and his family?

Would he ever truly find out? And would the house finally get some rest – would he finally get some rest? Tomorrow just might bring some answers thought Pietre as he turned off the light and drifted off to sleep with various extravagant ways of proposing to Sylvia jostling for position in his mind.

Chapter 23.

Over the next few days many things had begun to take shape and today, maybe, they would all get a few more answers. Harold and Pietre had discussed the takeover of the Hendrickson Corporation and, barring any unforeseen events, that should be completed within the week. Sylvia was due to fly out to England on Saturday as the Doctor's had assured her that her Father's condition was stable – for now. Pietre could not wait to see Sylvia again. He had arranged for her to stay with Harold and Maud at their delightful cottage just along the road from the farmhouse. Pietre desperately wanted Sylvia to like Saham Toney as much as he did. What if she hated it? What would he do then? Surely she would love the place as much as he did? Pietre realised that he was being irrational. He was wound up that was all – after all it wasn't every day a chap asked the girl of his dreams to be his wife was it? What if she said no? Oh my God! What then? Don't be such a bloody fool thought Pietre as he opened the door of his bedroom and went downstairs.

The sky was cloudless and the birds were in full voice as Pietre came down for breakfast. He paused, only briefly, as he entered the kitchen. Today was going to be a better day. Today HAD to be a better day. As he looked around at the sea of expectant faces looking towards him Pietre smiled. And for the first time in a long time his smile reached his eyes. Pietre sensed that something exceptional could happen today. Quite what he did not know for sure – but he knew it would be eventful to say the least.

It had been arranged that everyone connected with the events of the last few months would gather at the farmhouse later that morning. The Police had assured everyone that, as far as they could ascertain, Elijah had fled. There had been an extensive search of the area and it had been agreed that Elijah had disappeared from the area for good. A massive Police search throughout the nation would soon catch up with him. He didn't have the intelligence, or the means, to evade capture for much longer. The Police presence at the house would continue for the foreseeable future but the Police had assured them, as best they could, that they were as safe as they could possibly be- considering. No-one in the house truly believed that, of course, but they all made the right noises for the benefit of the Authorities. It had been agreed, for the time being at least, that Thomas and Grace would go to visit their Uncle Seb in his new home in London. The kids had been reluctant at first but had acceded eventually. No doubt slightly influenced by the opportunity for some serious retail therapy as promised by Elspeth. No-one voiced their real concerns for the safety of the children It didn't need voicing.

The children were dispatched by taxi later that morning. To say it was a strained goodbye was a real understatement. The kids were no fools but, faced with such a united front, they reluctantly agreed to spend the week away in London. Wouldn't it be a marvellous opportunity for them both to catch up with their old school chums and tell them all about their amazing trip to Paris after all?

The Reverend Wellbeloved stood in front of the hall mirror and took stock. He had spoken, at length, with Maud regarding the house and its "presence".

As a religious man Adam Wellbeloved was in a real quandary. He knew that Maud was struggling with the events of recent times. He knew that it had taken a great deal of courage and fortitude to ask him for his help. He had, very reluctantly, agreed to keep his visit a secret from his Bishop. "Just for the time being eh?" Maud had asked him earnestly. As he took one last look at his reflection Adam Wellbeloved was glad that he had decided to settle here in Saham Toney. He had serious reservations at first but now realised that, to paraphrase, God did move in mysterious ways. Adam double checked everything he needed was with him and strode out to his car. What would happen? He did not know but what he did know was that he would do everything he possibly could to help heal the crisis of faith that his good friend Maud was experiencing. He hoped too that this could be the start of a long and fruitful relationship with the rest of the Carrington clan.

Oscar Washington was both excited and terrified in equal measure. He had been both surprised and unnerved by the telephone conversation he had had with Pieter. What possible use could he be to them all? Oh! He knew that he had gleaned a not inconsiderable amount of information regarding the farmhouse. But why did they need him there? With the photocopy of the original drawings of the floor plan for "Haven's Retreat" tucked under his arm Oscar began his journey. He had been booked into the pub run by Gordon and Mavis but upon hearing the reason why he wouldn't be staying there now Oscar's resolve almost deserted him. What had he got himself involved in eh? Whatever it was, thought Oscar, he had never felt so alive and so needed! Bring it on as the young ones say nowadays laughed Oscar to himself as he headed for the train station.

Gordon Jarvis, however, was not certain he had the stomach or the nerve for today. He did not like visiting the farmhouse. He did not like going into that room. What he did not like even less, however, was his cowardice. He had never knowingly backed away from a situation before but he had never been in a situation like this before had he? As he wondered all this Mavis came up behind him and gently squeezed his arm. No words passed between them – no words were necessary- but both of them knew that this situation needed to be resolved for everyone's sake. Their lives had been dramatically affected by "Haven's Retreat" before and now more than ever. The pub would reopen, eventually, and everything would get back to some semblance of normality, but right now the priority was the house and its secrets. Gordon had vehemently insisted that Mavis stay away from the farmhouse that day and, for once, Mavis knew when she was beaten.

Harold had woken that morning very early. He had lain in bed watching his adored wife as she slept. Maud had not slept well recently and Harold was glad to see, whilst sleeping at least, she did not have that slightly haunted, frightened look about her. He loved her so completely and he knew that if they could, somehow, get through today then maybe things would be okay. Could they get through today? If ex Major Harold Carrington had anything to do with it then, of course, they could get through it.

Maud, meanwhile, had been feigning sleep for the past hour. She knew how concerned Harold and the rest of the family were for her. She was concerned for herself too.

Her faith was on the line right now and she fervently hoped with all of her heart that it would not be found lacking. As she heard Harold climb down the stairs Maud prepared herself for battle. Oh she had no doubt that a battle it would be! As she surveyed herself in the not very forgiving bathroom mirror Maud voiced her concerns out loud.

It was not something that she usually did but today was also something that she didn't usually do either! "Right old girl. Put your war paint on, Get you armour on and let's go into battle eh?"

Everyone assembled in the lounge of "Haven's Retreat" was doing their utmost to avoid each other's eyes. Oh! The forced bravado and camaraderie would have looked genuine to an outsider but everyone in the room knew just how false and strained it all was. Finally, Pietre could stand it no longer. Slowly and deliberately he rose from his chair, cleared his throat, looked at every face there individually and spoke.

"Thank you everyone for being here. I realise how difficult it must be for you all. I know I speak for all of us when I say that this terrible situation cannot and will not continue. I took the liberty of asking you all here so that we can all discuss just what has happened; what is still happening, here.

Gordon, would you mind telling us all about the events of last year please? I know it is difficult and I know none of us want to face up to the terrible things that we have all gone through but we need to get to the bottom of all this – don't we?"

For the next few hours everyone was totally honest about everything.

Oscar Washington had unveiled the original floor plan for the farmhouse and it was discovered that the part of the house that was now the office – the part of the house where EVERYONE hated to be had originally been where the grand fireplace had stood in the hallway. It had been changed many years before Oscar had said, according to his humble opinion. Oscar had taken the liberty of looking in the office when he had first arrived to get his bearings and he was convinced that he was right. The grand fireplace was indeed now the office.

The Reverend Wellbeloved had spoken then. He had admitted, eventually, under the very direct questioning of Harold that he had listened to many of his Parishioners who had come to him with their concerns and troubles after the truly awful events at the pub. As a man of God it troubled the Reverend that all of the people he had spoken to had told him almost the same thing – and that was that many, many years ago it was rumoured that a truly abhorrent event had taken place at the wedding of the first owners of the farmhouse. Everyone had dismissed most of what they knew as myth and legend – something that had grown more and more outlandish and fiendish with every generation adding juicy bits to make it even more shocking and terrible! Now, however, there was reason to believe that not everything that had been handed down had been a complete fabrication.

After the Reverend had told them of what he knew, or rather, what he had been told was the truth; no-one spoke for quite a while. Surely this could not have happened here in this house? That sort of thing didn't really happen – did it?

Over the next few hours Gordon, Mavis, Gerry and a very reluctant Elspeth had all admitted to feeling SOMETHING about the office wasn't right. Oh! No-one had seen anything at all. No-one had seen a headless man with his head in his hands, wrapped in a white sheet and with chains rattling behind him. Nothing like that. No-one had seen anything but they had all FELT something. No-one could quantify what it was but, nevertheless, they all felt the same about the room.

Harold had remained quiet for most of the morning. He was still struggling to come to terms with it all. Stuff and nonsense! Stuff and nonsense!

When Maud and Elspeth had gone into the kitchen to prepare coffee Harold had made his excuses about going into the cellar to get the wine for the evening meal. In truth Harold wanted and needed to go into the office and see for himself what all the fuss was about. He was a military man and had never walked away from a battle before and he had no intentions of backing away now!

As he slowly, and quietly, turned the key to the office Harold was both annoyed and perplexed to discover that his heart was racing and he felt both hot and cold at the same time. Pull yourself together you old fool chided Harold to himself as he carefully shut the door behind himself.

Harold surveyed the room. If this was indeed the former grand hallway then where would the fireplace have been? Surely there must be some evidence of its whereabouts in this room? Harold methodically went around the room trying to figure out just where this so called fireplace might be but without the detailed plan that Oscar had brought with him he could not be certain where to look. Harold realised, for now, that his search was over. For now that is. He must get back to the others before they wondered where he had gotten to. Just as silently Harold closed the door and went down to the cellar.

Harold sensed, rather than saw, something when he was done in the cellar. He had never realised that the office was, in fact, directly above the main body of the wine cellar .He had never noticed that before but .then again, he had never needed to know before had he? Just what secrets did the house have to tell he mused? The logical soldier in him tried to dismiss these thoughts but the inquisitive human part of him wanted answers. This house had caused much heartache for many people and if they could get to the bottom of all this then surely that must be a good thing eh? With that thought Harold picked the wine he needed and went back to the others. Now was not the right time but it would be soon enough!

Harold Carrington was not the soldier he once thought he was thought Maud as she covertly watched her beloved Husband as he returned from the cellar. Harold's precise military mind knew exactly where the wine he needed for tonight could be found and it would not have taken anything like as long to discover as Harold had been away!

What was he up to wondered Maud to herself as she busied herself in the kitchen? She did not know for certain but, by goodness, she would find out or her name was not Maud Carrington. Poor Harold did not realised just what questions lay ahead for him that night.

Chapter 24.

Lunchtime brought with it a certain respite from the worries of the day. The "girls" as Gerry had referred to Elspeth and Maud had done them all proud with a delightful lunch that had taken on a slightly different tone as the Policeman on duty to guard them had also been invited to eat with them. That poor man must not be forgotten insisted Maud as she ushered the bemused Constable into a chair with strict instructions to eat up dear ringing in his ears.

Everyone around the kitchen table was lost in their own thoughts about what had been discovered and discussed that morning. Oscar Washington had staked his not inconsiderable reputation on the certainty that Elijah Stump was a direct descendant of Lizzie Stump who, even if only a small part of her infamy were true, was indeed a witch! When he had spoken this out loud for the first time Oscar had been surprised that no-one had laughed at him! Surely no sensible person believed in such things today – did they? As he had looked around the lounge at the faces of the people he had come to know a little Oscar realised that not only everyone else in the room thought like that but that he did so too!

Witchcraft! Bloody witchcraft! Whatever next? The Reverend Wellbeloved had studied his shoes for a not inconsiderable time as he battle with both his faith and his own slight disbelief. Surely this could not be true? Could it? The church had long been in battle with so called Witchcraft. The subject had been a contentious one during his training and many people much higher in the Church than himself, whilst not completely disowning the possibility of it , had actively discouraged the subject to be discussed. The power of good over evil was one that had been waged for centuries and would continue to be battle for centuries to come. But not here, not now, in his little village! Surely not?

As he looked up from his shoes he caught Maud's expression. She was a lady struggling with all of this. What should he do?

Pietre hardly tasted his food as his mind was in such a state of turmoil. What had he done? He had arrived in this beautiful village and caused untold havoc and distress to these people sitting around this table. He would never forgive himself - for that he was sure of. What he was also sure about was his conviction that, somehow, the key to all of these troubles lay in this house and he would do everything in his power to make it right for these lovely people. How the hell he was going to do that he had absolutely no idea!

As the night began to draw in the mood in the house had improved. Oscar had said that he would research as much as he could about the so called "vendetta" within the village. The Reverend Wellbeloved had agreed to contact the family of the poor woman who had died to see if they could come up with ANYTHING that might help put an end to this misery and everyone agreed that it was time for the Police to be informed that they all thought the services of a Policeman guarding them 24 hours an day was no longer needed. Thank you very much. Gerry had been cajoled into telephoning the Police Station first thing in the morning and had, reluctantly, agreed to do so. Elspeth said that she would tell the children some of the things that had been discussed – but not all. It would not do to worry them unduly –would it?

As they all said there goodnights it had not escaped anyone's notice that the office, and what should be done about it, had not been discussed. What the hell could be done eh? Tomorrow was another day after all and arrangements had been made for everyone to return tomorrow to see what the next step should be. As the Carrington's said goodbye to their guests and wished them well until tomorrow none of them could see Elijah Stump sitting high up in a tree directly across from the front door. Oh! They were all coming back tomorrow were they? As he digested this information the little voice inside his head began to whisper, began to cajole, and began to flatter Elijah. As the voices plans for tomorrow entered the subconscious mind of the pathetic Elijah who, by this time, had absolutely no control over his actions or the wishes of the malevolent Lizzie Stump Elijah had absolutely no idea of the catastrophic events that would unfold.

-

Chapter 25.

Sylvia Hendrickson took a long and dispassionate look at herself in the bathroom mirror. What she saw disappointed her. All she saw were the lines etched around her eyes and the dark circles that seemed to be growing daily. Her Father's health had stabilised for now but she knew, in her heart of hearts, that he would soon be gone from her. What would she do then she wondered? Which direction would her life go in? Would Pietre be a part of her new life? All these thoughts, and many more besides, threatened to weaken her already fragile resolve. Pietre loved her, of that she was sure. Why else would he insist that she fly over to England when he must know what a difficult time this was for her? The Company that her Father had started was going through an incredibly difficult phase just now and she had spent an agonising amount of time debating the validity of leaving the country.

As she walked into the Head Office of the Corporation she literally ran into Ludvig Ahlstedt the most senior member of the Board. Sylvia had always mistrusted the man. Oh! He had always been most polite and almost servile in his dealings with her and yet, and yet, there was just something about the man that made her flesh crawl. "My dear Sylvia, so good to see you, and looking so well!" Ahlstedt always spoke in this slimy sycophantic way to her and now was not an exception! Sylvia could not bring herself to look at this odious man and quickly made her excuses and went into her office where she very pointedly said in a loud voice that she must not be disturbed for any reason. She hoped that that might give her some respite from the constant questioning about the state of her Father and the state of the Company. She realised that the Staff were concerned about their jobs etc. but right now she could not deal with any of that. What she needed to do was clear her head before she arrived in the little village in England that Pietre had told her about. She so wanted to surprise Pietre and she just hoped he would be pleased to see her. She had spoken at length to her beloved Father as he had been the one to insist that she go to Pieter immediately and that she was not to waste another second of her life wondering what to do for the best. Her Father had promised her that he would do his best not to die whilst she was away. When he had said those words Sylvia had been unable to speak for a long moment until she felt the thin, aged hand of her Father grip her arm with a fierce energy that belied the fragile state of his health. He had fixed her with his piercing blue eyes and she had been unable or unwilling, to tear herself away as she listened to her Father's impassioned plea for her to go this very day and not to come home without that young man she so obviously thought the world of. He had also said out loud, for the first and only time, that he was aware that he was dying but his dying would be all the more bearable if he was to know that Sylvia had the chance of happiness and had the love of a good man. He explained that he had had an awful lot of time on his hands lying in his sick bed and he had come to the inevitable conclusion that he was a stubborn old goat who, if he wasn't extremely careful, would be responsible for his Daughter's unhappiness. Sylvia and her Father had hugged each other with a sense of urgency and Sylvia had left her Father's bedroom without daring to look at his face. She did not trust her resolve if she had seen any sort of distress on the old man's face and so she had beaten a hasty retreat.

No was the time for action if she was to have even the slightest chance of happiness!

Elizabeth, her trusted Secretary, produced a cup of coffee from nowhere almost before Sylvia had taken her coat off! What would she do without Elizabeth thought Sylvia? – Not for the first time.

A little over two hours later and she was in the Company limousine heading for the Airport feeling a lot less concerned than at the start of the day. Elizabeth had assured her that she was more than capable of running the Company for a few days whilst she was in England. "Running the Company eh?" laughed Sylvia as Elizabeth strode purposefully towards her desk. The look that Elizabeth had given her had stopped Sylvia in her tracks! She had had no doubts then about leaving her post. There were telephones, computers, fax machines etc. in Norfolk. Weren't there?

Pietre had been most insistent about meeting her at Heathrow Airport. He simply would not take no for an answer. Besides, Pietre had said that he had some business to attend to in the City and he had also said that he wanted her all to himself for a day as he had some things he needed to discuss with her! SOME THINGS. SOME THINGS! Sylvia hoped that if he was going to propose, which she desperately hoped he was going to do, then she did not want them itemising as SOME THINGS like any other business on a meeting's agenda.

She would have a little word in his ear if he thought that that was the right way to go about things. And make no mistake! The thought of Pietre made her smile. The thought of Pietre always made her smile she mused as the limousine sped silently towards the Airport. Her flight would get into Heathrow quite late and Sylvia had been just a little disappointed to realise that Pietre would not be meeting her until the next day. He had assured her that when he did arrive they had so much to discuss that he wondered if she minded if they stayed one night in the London hotel before heading to Norfolk. It all sounded very intriguing and Sylvia's stomach did a little flutter at what might be happening to her and Pietre. She knew she would just have to wait – but not long now!

Pietre, meanwhile, did not have any time for such musings as he spoke hurriedly and urgently to Elizabeth in Stockholm. Elizabeth had telephoned him, as he had requested, the instant Sylvia had left Head Office and he had grilled her regarding the final preparations for the emergency Board Meeting that was to be set up next week. Elizabeth, however, failed to elaborate as to the exact whereabouts of Sylvia and she was more than a little pleased that Pietre seemed a little distracted and did not pursue the matter any further!

Pietre had, with the invaluable help of Harold, managed to purchase a controlling interest in the Hendrickson Corporation by buying up the Shares of most of the other Board Members. Some members had been avoided as Elizabeth assured him that they aligned themselves with Ludvig Ahlstedt and could not, therefore, be trusted to keep it a secret. Pietre had realised just how bad things had got within the Corporation when it had proved comparatively easy to purchase Shares.

The Board members willing to sell had not been so naïve as to accept Pieter's first offer however and Pietre had needed to allocate even more funds than he had first envisaged- but he knew that he was doing the right thing; he just hoped that Sylvia would see it that way! Oh well thought Pietre – too late now!

Harold, Maud and the rest of the Carrington family were already seated around the large kitchen table as Pieter entered the kitchen. The smell of bacon assailed his nostrils and Pietre realised just how hungry he was! "Now, young man, as Harold would no doubt say – an Army marches into battle on a full stomach. Isn't that right Harold" As she realised what she had said Maud was both embarrassed and annoyed with herself. Why had she said that? What was she thinking – talking about battles like that?

Pietre, as usual, came to her rescue by simply thanking her for thinking of his stomach. He had not really eaten properly for days he had said. "And that probably goes for all of us eh?"

After breakfast, which everyone wolfed down, they all retired to the sitting room. No-one had suggested that they go into the office just yet- and for that everyone was grateful. Oh! They all knew that the office situation needed to be addressed. But not just now eh?

Elspeth was the first to speak.

"Gordon, Oscar and the Reverend Wellbeloved will be here shortly and I think it best to wait until everyone is assembled before we decide what to do next. Is everyone agreed?" A sea of faces greeted her little speech with varying degrees of uncertainty and anxiety but everyone did agree that it was probably the best thing to do. Time seemed to drag on for an eternity as they all sat waiting. How could time go so slowly?

Eventually everyone was relieved to hear the sound of a car pulling up to the house. Maud took it upon herself to be the one to open the door and she ushered them all in with almost indecent haste!

After the stilted greetings were over Pietre stood in the centre of the room and spoke.

"Thank you everyone for putting yourselves through this. I, for one, am deeply grateful and I need to apologise again for all the hurt and distress me coming here has brought to you all. I think that we are all in agreement that SOMETHING is going on in this house. I have absolutely no idea what that might be but I am grateful for all your support." Pieter's nerve almost got the better of him just then and he was grateful when Harold spoke next.

Harold cleared his throat before he spoke. This was going to be difficult for everyone but especially for him. He had always rubbished the idea of ghosts, ghoulies and witchcraft before – but not now!

"As most of you are already aware I have always been very sceptical about the notion of spirits etc. but I must confess that after the other evening I am now not so sure. If you remember I excused myself from your company on the pretext of fetching some wine from the cellar. That was a lie.

I went into the office to see, or rather, sense for myself what all the fuss was about. I will tell you now that I, personally, felt no evidence of a presence in the room. However, when I went down to the cellar - things felt very different. Now the cellar is directly underneath the office and when I was in there I did sense something. What the dickens it was I have absolutely no idea- but there was something unnerving about that cellar that night. Oscar, you said that you had a copy of the original floor plan didn't you? Well I suggest that we look at that floor plan now and try to determine just exactly where on it the office now stands. It's a start anyway. Everyone in agreement? Good. Then let's start eh?"

And so it was that everyone gathered around the large dining table and began to peruse the copy of the original floor plan. As they looked at it they formulated a rough estimate as to the whereabouts of what must have been the original fireplace. The dimensions of the hall suggested that it was a grand affair and the office now occupied a particular spot along a wall that had, many years ago, been removed.

The Reverend Wellbeloved reiterated what the villagers had been telling him about the terrible tragedy that had taken place all those years ago in the hallway of "Haven's Retreat" and so it was agreed that they would start looking there for some evidence. Quite what they were expecting to find was anyone's guess but it was agreed that that was as good a place to start as any.

When Gerry turned the key in the door of the office you could have heard a pin drop. Everyone in the farmhouse was on pins. Oh! They all realised that they would hardly be confronted by a weeping, wailing ghost – but what would they be confronted with?

The office felt unnatural cold and unfriendly – to say the least! Slowly, using the floor plan copy they located where they all agreed was the most likely place to search. What they were searching for was anyone's guess.

Harold, with his usual military manner took control and began to move filing cabinets and other paraphernalia away from one particular section of wall.

Gordon, meanwhile, was having real difficulty in remaining in the room. Don't be so bloody stupid he thought to himself. Just what the hell was he so frightened of? As he looked at everyone else he squared his shoulders and prepared himself. For what he had no idea but he had walked away from difficult decisions before- and look where that had got him. He had almost lost his children for good when he had first fled to the farmhouse. He had helped his beloved wife to commit suicide by allowing her to store up sufficient painkillers to put herself out of her misery. His children had disowned him at first but, thanks to all the incredible people he had met when he first arrived he had made contact with his children again and they were all trying to build bridges. He would be forever grateful for all the support he had received from them and now was the time to, somehow, pay them back for looking out for him. If he could, somehow, make things right for all the people standing in this room then, surely that were a good thing?

"Gerry? I think we might need to break down some of this wall. Don't you? Do you have a lump hammer or something in the barn we could use? You don't mind if we knock a hole in this wall do you? I really think that we need to see as much as we can of the original layout. Does everyone agree?"

Gerry was the first to break the silence. "I wouldn't be bothered if you knocked the whole bloody thing down I don't mind telling you!" I will take great personal pleasure in helping to obliterate the damned room. Anyone else up for a bit of recreational vandalism?"

No one spoke. No one said a word.

"Young man! I know that this is a difficult situation we have found ourselves in but LANGUAGE! "

As she took stock of the faces around her Maud Carrington began to giggle. As she giggled the atmosphere in the room changed. Suddenly everyone began to laugh. It was laughter generated by fear, anxiety and tension but it was a blessed relief for everyone as they all became slightly hysterical.

Gordon broke the strange reverie by announcing that he would go, right now, and fetch anything and everything he could lay his hands on from the barn. He only jokingly enquired as to whether Gerry had a J.C.B tucked somewhere in a forgotten corner. The look of confusion on Pieter's face threatened to start the girls off again with the more than slightly hysterical laughter but one stern look from Harold was enough to quell both his Wife and His Daughter.

And so it was that Gordon was dispatched outside to rummage in the barn for anything suitable whilst Oscar and the Reverend were told to "Roll up your sleeves Gentlemen and let's get to work!" by Harold who was back in charge.

Elijah could hardly believe his luck. That bloke from the pub had just rushed outside as though his life depended on it and he had left the door to the kitchen open!

Now was his chance. Now he could get into the house. What was he waiting for?

 Lizzie's voice began to invade his mind again. That bloody woman! Would she never give him a minute's peace? He knew that the only possible way for him to ever experience peace again was after he had killed the blonde stranger. Now was the time. Now he was finally close to getting rid of Lizzie Stump once and for all. Slowly and stealthily Elijah crept towards the house. As he entered through the door to the kitchen he could hear the sounds of voices coming from another part of the house. Now he knew which way to go he inched his way silently towards the sounds. He was within a few feet of the door when he heard the sound of Gordon coming back shouting that he had found a veritable arsenal of tools and it would take them no time at all to demolish the wall and see what secrets it might reveal?

Elijah almost cried out as a searing pain shot through his head. Lizzie was screaming at him. He could not make out what she was trying to say and then he realised! She was not speaking to him but she had begun to chant. The chant started slowly and quietly in his head but with every passing second it became louder, more intense and more filled with hatred. Elijah just wanted it to stop. Please stop for f#### sake! Why won't it stop? Just let it stop! Elijah Stump knew that NOW was the time for it to stop. NOW was the time to kill the blonde stranger. As he crept every closer to the door Elijah's grip tightened on the shotgun he had brought with him. Lizzie guided him towards the sound of the voices and he was within inches of the door when he heard the sound of Gordon's voice.

"I've found plenty of tools in the barn for all of us. Right, let's get started eh?"

Gordon passed within inches of Elijah who had hidden just behind the main staircase. He was only a few feet away. How the hell had that stupid man missed him mused Elijah as a giggle threatened to engulf him. People were so stupid sometimes and that man's stupidity would cost them all dearly.

Inside the office everyone was completely unaware that Elijah was standing less than 20 feet away. Gordon could be heard handing out tools and some posh sounding older bloke was giving orders out. Pompous idiot! Suddenly the sound of female voices was heard and Elijah's resolve began to weaken. What the hell were women doing in there?

The sound of a foreign voice brought Elijah back to reality. That voice! That voice could only belong to one person.

The blonde stranger.

Without stopping to think Elijah opened the door.

Chapter 26.

No-one noticed for a second that the door to the office had opened. Suddenly the sound of screaming filled the tiny room. Maud had let out an ear piercing sound as she realised that the stranger in front of her was carrying a gun!

Elijah looked around him at the various people in front of him. He recognised most of them from seeing them around the village. There was the self- important Vicar, there was that bloke from the pub, the posh older couple who thought they were somebody along with the folks from London who had come to the village and started all this trouble. Oh! He couldn't wait to deal with all of them, but they would have to wait. He knew who he was looking for all right! As he scanned the room he did not see Oscar Washington out of the corner of his eye.

 Oscar had been kneeling behind a filing cabinet that had been moved away from the wall to allow some access when Elijah first burst into the room.

Oscar realised immediately that he must remain hidden. How he knew that he was unsure of but he knew he MUST remain hidden!

Lizzie, meanwhile, had begun to speak to Elijah – or rather she had begun to scream at him!

Slowly and deliberately Elijah closed the door behind him and smiled. He had seen the blonde stranger and he was less than 10 feet away from him! This would be SO easy and, at last, he would be free from the voices.

The silence in the room was unbearable. No-one had uttered a word.

 Elijah stood with his back to the door and looked each and every one of his victims in the eye before he spoke. The stupid old woman was being comforted by the younger woman. Quite attractive she was too! Mused Elijah. Lizzie screeched at him to concentrate and so, with more than a little reluctance, he continued his perusal of the inhabitants of the room. The older posh bloke was squaring his shoulders as though he was about to move towards him. With just the merest movement of the gun at his side Elijah was pleased to see that a flicker of doubt crossed the face of the old man. Maybe the old bugger knew when he was beaten eh? Laughed Elijah to himself. And then there was the odious and hateful Reverend Wellbeloved! As he held his gaze the hatred poured out of Elijah. It took what was left of his own willpower not to simply blow that man's head off right here and now. The Stump's had avoided all contact with the clergy for as long as anyone could remember. THE BLOODY CLERGY. They had made his family's life a misery over the centuries, but now, that would all be sorted once and for all. Elijah would take great personal delight in eradicating the Reverend Wellbeloved from this earth and he hoped that he would endure a miserable existence in the afterlife, for wasn't that what all clergymen deserved?

The dreadful silence was broken by Pietre.

"What the hell are you doing here? Don't you know that the Police are looking for you? Don't you realise that the Police are here in the house- eh?" Pieter's blood froze in his veins as an unearthly cry emanated from the man with the gun.

Quietly and deliberately Elijah carefully explained that he knew all about the fact that they had dismissed the 24hour Police presence. He also told them that if ANYONE uttered another sound then he would not be responsible for what happened next. Did everyone understand? Did they all f****** understand?

At the sound of such profanity Maud bristled.

"Young man – you might be the one holding the gun right now but let me tell you something. Do not invade my Daughter's house and speak to me like that! Do you understand? Do you?" Elijah was totally unprepared for what happened next. That bloody woman was walking towards him! What the hell did she think she was doing?

The incredible noise of a gun being fired in such a confined space was terrifying – to say the least, but when the smoke cleared Elijah noted that everyone looked at him in a different light. They knew that he was in charge. They knew that, he, Elijah Stump was in charge!

Oscar Washington had NEVER been more scared in his entire life. What the hell was happening? Who was this man?

Maud, Harold, Gerry, Elspeth, Gordon, The Reverend Wellbeloved and Pietre looked aghast at the gaping hole that had appeared in the wall not 3 feet away from the prone figure of Oscar Washington. Pietre was convinced that the dear man must be dead. He was not moving! He was not moving! What the hell was going on?

Lizzie, meanwhile, had not had such fun for a very long time. Oh! How she was enjoying herself. She had not had fun for how long exactly? Several hundred years or more it would seem. This little bit of news tickled Lizzie and so she began to giggle like a naughty schoolgirl.

The sight and sound of the completely deranged man laughing hysterically before them was the last straw as far as Harold was concerned. He could not, and would not, allow this terrible ordeal to go on for a moment longer. He had no choice but to try to disarm this crazy individual. Just as he was about to move towards Elijah Harold saw an almost imperceptible shake of the head by Gerry whose eyes went down to the floor where Oscar lay.

Oscar Washington was not a violent man. He was not what could be described in any way, shape or form as "macho" but what Oscar did possess was a deep rooted sense of right and wrong. How dare this man threaten these lovely people? How dare he threaten to undermine all the hard work he himself had done in collating the history of this beautiful, but disturbed, place?

Lizzie began to speak again.

"You. You over there. Do you have any idea who I am eh? Do you?"

Pietre knew with absolute and mortifying certainty that the voice was addressing him. The voice did not seem to belong to the man standing in front of them. It did not seem to belong to any human that he had ever heard speak.

"What do you want from me? What is it you want?" Pieter's voice sounded more controlled than he himself felt. He knew, somehow, that if he showed any sign of weakness then he would pay a terrible price for it.

"You have absolutely no idea who I am? Do you?" laughed Lizzie. Oh! How she was enjoying this.

"I do not know who you are but what I do know is that you can't hurt me. You can't hurt me because you are already dead! Right? Right?"

Elijah's face began to contort into almost indescribable positions and his body began to tremble violently. When he opened his eyes and snarled at everyone in the room Elspeth began to quietly cry. Gerry put a protective arm around her just as Elijah began to rock back and forth. As Elijah's attention was held by Pietre Gerry very carefully began to slide a crowbar sideways towards the silent figure of Oscar Washington. Harold noticed this and began to position himself in front of Maud and in doing so blocked the very real chance that Elijah might just see what was going on.

Pieter, meanwhile, was having difficulty breathing.

Quietly at first the voices in his own head began to speak. What the hell was going on now? Pietre sensed, rather than heard, these sounds. Someone was trying to tell him something. What were they trying to tell him? None of this made any sense whatsoever. He was hearing voices now of all times. He was being held hostage with some of his dearest friends and he was hearing bloody voices!

The pure, unadulterated hatred that Lizzie felt for Pietre was her undoing in the end. She began to scream at Elijah. She began to scream so loudly that Elijah thought his head would burst. He could stand it no longer! He would not stand it a second longer.

Slowly and deliberately Elijah Stump raised the shotgun to his own head, opened his mouth, and put the shotgun there.

Maud and Elspeth screamed hysterically.

Gordon gasped and stepped forward.

Harold and Pieter held him back as they all stood silently watching this terrible scene unfold.

Elijah had never felt more tired than he did right now. He was past caring now. He just needed it to stop. He just wanted this living hell to end.

Lizzie continued to scream. She told Elijah that if he did this thing then his nightmare was only just beginning. She would be waiting for him on the other side. He thought that his earthly life was hell? It was going to get so much worse for him if he disobeyed Lizzie Stump.

In truth Lizzie was scared. Lizzie had never been scared once in her earthly or other life and she did not know what to do. Elijah Stump was the last remaining relative of the Stump clan. Why had he never had children? Why?

If he'd had children then things could have continued. As it was if the stupid man was to die then what would become of her? She would have no way of controlling the minds of anyone. There was no-one left to control if this idiot killed himself.

Elijah's hand trembled violently as he brought his finger ever closer to the trigger. Did he have the courage to do this? Did he want this torture to end? All it would take was one tiny squeeze and it would all be over.

Suddenly everything went black in Elijah's head.

Chapter 27.

Oscar Washington stood in disbelief and horror as he looked at what he had done.

He had crept up behind that maniac and hit him on the head with the crowbar.

He had hit him HARD.

Chaos ensued for the next few moments.

Harold and Gordon had pounced on the prone figure of Elijah as Gerry had raced into the barn to fetch some strong rope. They had quickly tied him up. Elijah continued to writhe about. How the hell was he still doing that after Oscar had never nearly caved his head in?

Lizzie was incandescent with suffused rage. That idiot boy! How could he kill Pietre now? He needed to kill him so that Lizzie could exact her revenge on his odious family for all that they had done to her and her family so long ago.

She would not let this happen if it was the last thing she ever did.

Summoning all of her not inconsiderable power Lizzie began to chant.

She had never had the courage to recite this chant before.

Starting quietly she began.

With every passing second the chant became louder and louder until, with supreme satisfaction, Lizzie realised that everyone in the room could hear her!

Everyone!

It was working. It was actually working. She had never dared to hope before that it might work. She knew that this was her last possible hope. She had been warned that this chant could only be performed once. If it failed she would be condemned for ever.

She must make it work! She must make it work!

The Reverend Wellbeloved knew, instinctively, that he was in the presence of pure evil.

Maud and Elspeth began to cry and hug each other for comfort. Harold simply stood to attention and looked straight ahead! He had absolutely no idea what was going on but he admitted, only to himself mind, that he had never been as scared during battle as he was right now.

Gerry and Gordon held each other's gaze for a fraction of a second before once more securing the prone body of Elijah Stump.

The noise in the small room began to increase in both volume and malice. How a sound could be malicious no-one in the room knew, but the malevolence emanating from that sound was truly terrifying.

The Reverend Wellbeloved knew what he must do.

He must face the Devil head on in this room.

Adam Wellbeloved stood impassively above the convulsing form of Elijah Stump and very gently, and deliberately, placed his hands on the heart of the poor creature lying before him. The howl of anguish and despair that came from that poor soul almost broke Adam's resolve.

Almost – but not quite.

Adam began to recite from memory. He began to recite quietly at first and then he became louder and louder until he was matching the sounds Elijah was making decibel for decibel.

Lizzie was more terrified than ever. She was losing her grip on Elijah. She was losing her grip on herself.

She was screaming louder than she ever thought possible.

Slowly, and inexorably, Adam began to win the battle.

Slowly, and surely, Lizzie's voice became quieter and more subdued.

Slowly, and surely, Elijah began to hear less and less of Lizzie.

He realised, with awful clarity, that he would spend the rest of his days rotting in some awful prison for the crimes he had committed.

The unfairness of the situation hit him then. This was not his fault. None of this was his fault? Surely everyone would see that? Surely?

An overwhelming rage began to grow inside the mind of the hapless Elijah.

It was all the fault of that bloody woman Lizzie!

Well, this time, he would not let her take charge. He had had enough. If it was the last thing that he did he would rid himself of Lizzie Stump once and for all!

With superhuman strength he did know he possessed Elijah sprang up.

Pieter looked Elijah in the eyes and held his gaze.

Without any comprehension of what on earth he was saying Pietre began to speak. Slowly and quietly at first Pietre began to chant just like Lizzie had been doing - but this chant was different somehow. This chant began to have an incredible influence on the atmosphere within this tiny space. It was almost as if the room was alive! It was as if the room was full of, if not people, then the spirits of people. Pietre had never really understood what people meant when they claimed to have been possessed by the Devil – but My God – he knew EXACTLY what they must have felt like.

Everyone in the room stood transfixed as the chanting continued. Gordon seemed to retreat inside himself with every passing moment. Maud and Elspeth clung to each other and sobbed whilst their Husbands slowly and deliberately put their arms around them and tried to protect them both as best they could. What the hell they were protecting them from they had absolutely no idea.

As the noise levels within such a confined space became almost unbearable the energy within the room began to change. The sense of utter evil began to permeate the very walls of the office.

The animosity and loathing for Pieter poured out of every pore in Elijah's body.

He had had enough of being controlled by other people. By Lizzie stump and his useless Parent's.

He was in charge now!

He was in charge and he would be damned for all eternity if he didn't finish the job off once and for all.

Pieter never let his gaze fall from Elijah's face. Not for a second.

The voices inside Pieter's head had grown in both volume and clarity.

They were telling him all about the past and how his family had been so terribly wronged by the Stump's.

They were telling him that all his ancestors possessed the gift of "second sight" and that , if only he would allow it, he could and should , be a force to reckon with.

Time seemed to stand still for everyone in that room that day. Afterwards no-one could quite believe what had happened.

But happen it did!

Lizzie Stump and Flora Bromfield (nee Gibson.) stood facing each other several centuries after their mortal bodies had left this earth and eyed each other with contempt.

Flora's face did not display any emotion whatsoever and this unsettled Lizzie.

This unsettled Lizzie a lot!

Flora began to speak. Nervously at first but with ever more growing confidence.

"Lizzie, do you remember when we first met? I do. It was the morning of my wedding. And you said that nothing good could possibly come from this marriage. That was your first, big, mistake. Do you remember how you had me killed? I do. On my Daughter's wedding day. I was stabbed and left to bleed to death right here on this very spot. Surely you must remember that eh? You have always assumed that you had won. Haven't you. Or have you?

Where are you right now eh? Hoping with your last breath that this pathetic mortal will do your bidding one final time. Truly pathetic."

As Lizzie listened to the ever more confident Flora doubts crept, unasked for, into her mind

.She, Lizzie Stump, had always been in control.

ALWAYS.

Flora continued as if she had not noticed the change in Lizzie. But she had noticed the change and she knew what she must do.

"You have always believed that your evil way is the only way. Right?"

Pieter/ Flora did not give Elijah/Lizzie chance to reply.

"That has been your downfall from the beginning and will continue to be your downfall right until the end. Which, if I have my way, will be very soon? Very soon indeed! You may have not actually murdered my Parent's on this very spot all those years ago but we both know that it was you. Wasn't it?

WASN'T IT?

The ferocity in Flora's voice had an astonishing effect on Lizzie/Elijah. Lizzie did not know what to do in the face of the venom in Flora's voice.

"What you failed to realise Lizzie is that I am as determined as you are. Your evil will not be allowed to win don't you see? Look around you Lizzie.

LOOK! I said! What do you see Lizzie? Tell me, what do you see?"

Lizzie/Elijah began to feel nervous. Neither knew what to do. As their gaze went slowly around the room a terrible sense of foreboding gripped them.

Elijah began to whimper as his eyes found Pietre/Flora. The look of steely determination was one of the last things Elijah Stump remembered before he struck with awesome and lethal force.

Elspeth Carrington had NEVER been more afraid than she was at this precise moment. Elijah had grabbed her and was pressing the shotgun hard into her neck! Her distraught Parents could only look on in horror as Elijah began to back towards the door. The Reverend Wellbeloved prayed like he had never prayed before. Oscar Washington wondered how he was still standing up- he was so frightened. Gordon, meanwhile, had other emotions coursing through his veins. Without waiting to think he launched himself with every ounce of his energy and hit Elijah full in the shoulder with all the strength he could muster.

A split second before Gordon made contact Elijah sensed what was about to happen. He sensed it but was just a fraction of a second to slow.

Gordon caught him slightly off balance and the two men fell with sickening force into the filing cabinet that had hidden Oscar Washington just a few moments ago. Elijah knew that, whatever happened, he must not relinquish his grip on the shotgun. He MUST finish the job.

The sound of the gun exploding for a second time within such a confined space was deafening!

Maud began to scream hysterically as Gordon staggered back covered in blood. Elspeth felt that she would pass out any moment but was saved by the gentle and strong arms of her beloved Gerry catching her as she fell. She felt a warm sensation down one side of her body and looked down to see that she was covered in blood also. So why, if she was covered in blood, did she not feel any pain? As her gaze swept around the room she let out a silent scream.

Elijah Stump lay on the ground with a smoking, gaping hole in his abdomen from which blood was spurting out at an alarming rate. The Reverend and Oscar were both trying desperately to stem the flow whilst Harold was on the telephone calling for an ambulance.

Pieter, meanwhile, was just staring into space. His lips were moving but no sound came from them as he rocked back and forth. As everyone's hearing began to return after the deafening noise from the gun they all realise that Pietre was praying.

Pietre was praying for the soul of Elijah!

Maud and Elspeth both took hold of a hand and began to pray silently together. The Reverend, Oscar and Gordon looked on in anguish as the life slowly and inexorably drifted away for Elijah.

Lizzie knew that this was the end. She knew that, somehow, she had lost. As the life ebbed away from Elijah- so the energy ebbed away from Lizzie. Oh! She tried to scream her venom one more time but to no avail.

When Elijah took his last earthly breath Lizzie realised that whatever hold she may have had over Elijah was gone.

Elijah Stump stood impassively surveying the scene before him. He knew that he was dead. He knew that as certainly as he knew anything. He looked down at the body before him and felt nothing. His earthly body had died but his spirit lived on! And what was more – he was now in charge!

No more ravings from Lizzie! At the thought of Lizzie Elijah surveyed the room looking for his nemesis! Where the hell was that bloody woman? She had made his life a complete misery for as long as he could remember and now it was payback time!

With intense satisfaction he caught sight of Lizzie cowering in the corner of the room that now stood on the exact spot where the murders had taken place all that time ago.

She looked bereft.

Not a flicker of emotion passed over the spirit face of Elijah Stump as he caught the eye of Lizzie. Without a word being spoken he headed away from the house without a backward glance.

Lizzie knew that her power was gone. She knew that she would never hold dominion over Elijah again – what she was not prepared for however was the sight that confronted her.

Flora and Joshua Bromfield stood before her in a terrible, mocking, parody of how they had stood so proudly that day. That day that should have been the happiest they had ever known. For a split second Lizzie felt a new set of emotions wash over her – only for a split second mind!

Regret, shame, remorse!

As the sound of Lizzie's manic laughter filled the room Flora, Joseph and so many of the others that Lizzie had been dreadful to – people she had not noticed at first and people she had not thought about –ever- began to walk slowly away until Lizzie realised that she was alone. She was truly alone for the first time in either her earthly or spirit life and she did not know what to do.

Abruptly the sound of Lizzie's laughter stopped as she suddenly found it difficult to get her breath. What the hell was happening to her? Why could she not breathe? Why could she not make a sound? Why did no-one want to help her?

As the spirit life of Lizzie Stump finally left her Elijah looked down, dispassionately, at her crumpled form. That bloody woman had brought him nothing but misery and torment all his life and he was glad to see the back of her because now HE WAS IN CHARGE.

As he looked at the retreating forms of Flora and Joshua little did they realise that, far from being over, their torment and the torment of the blonde fella had reached a new level. And this time revenge would be sweet – very sweet indeed!

Elijah was very comfortable with being in charge. Very comfortable indeed! All of his pathetic, earthly, life he had been overlooked. He had been mocked and ridiculed. He would not be mocked and ridiculed ever again! He would make certain of that. He might not be alive on earth but he sure as hell was alive in the spirit world and what was more he was revelling in his new found power and status. He had defeated Lizzie Stump and from the nervous looks from all of the other spirits gathered around he was a force to be reckoned with.

Flora and Joshua Bromfield, meanwhile, had plans of their own. They had won this particular battle and they had the advantage for now. How long this would last was anybody's guess. Elijah Stump had no relatives left but they doubted that that would stop him from continuing his vendetta against Pietre. Pietre was their own flesh and blood. Pietre might, naively, think that all this heartache was over now that Elijah had died but Flora and Joshua knew, with awful certainty that a new battle had just begun!

Chapter 28.

Pietre could not believe what had just happened. He had begun to hear voices for the very first time in his life and look what had happened! He stared down at the body of Elijah without really seeing him. His mind was in such turmoil. What the hell was going to happen now? A man had died! A man had died in this very room! Suddenly Pietre was aware of someone shaking his shoulders and asking him if he was okay.

Gordon Jarvis looked directly at Pietre without ever seeing him. The man was in total shock and as Pietre looked on Gordon began to crumple to the ground. Maud and Elspeth screamed that Gordon was dying and they needed the ambulance. NOW! Gerry said that Gordon was going to be okay, he had gone into shock- that was all.

THAT WAS ALL!

Maud began to shake. Her whole body was wracked with terrible tremors and she sat down heavily on the nearest chair.

Harold, meanwhile, had heard the sound of an approaching ambulance and he quietly left the room to let the Emergency Services in. As he stood in the doorway of "Haven's Retreat" it took all of his quite considerable willpower not to break down and cry. What he had just witnessed had been more shocking and terrifying than ANYTHING he had encountered during his long Army career.

What the hell had just happened?

The Emergency Services did an absolutely sterling job. The Police Officer sent to the house quickly ordered back up from Thetford. The room was sealed off for forensic reports and everyone was told to stay in the lounge until they could all be questioned about what had taken place.

The next morning and Maud stood in the kitchen making breakfast on auto pilot. She doubted that anyone would eat a morsel of the food she was preparing but she needed to keep herself busy. She wondered if any of them had had a wink of sleep that night. She knew that both she and Harold had not closed their eyes the entire night for fear of what their dreams would be. She and Harold had held hands and cried together. Her beloved Husband had, finally, admitted just how frightened her had been. He was certain that they were all going to die in that dreadful room. He was also certain that he would never set foot inside that damned room again if he lived to be a hundred. What the hell Gerry and Elspeth would do about that room, or indeed, about living in the house he was not sure but what he was absolutely certain of was that he would never feel the same about the place again!

Gerry and Elspeth had had a similar night themselves. They had not slept a wink. They had talked and cried throughout the night and had, eventually, come to a decision. They would demolish the room that had been the office. They would restore the hallway to what it had once been – or as near as anyone could get it- and they would not be driven out of their beautiful home by the awful events of that night.

They were both so glad that their beloved children had not been at home to witness the truly awful events of the previous night. Gerry had insisted that the children should know some of the things that had taken place but not all of them. He doubted, and Elspeth agreed, that they would know how to deal with the idea of evil spirits living within their home.

In the cold light of the morning it was almost as if the terrible events of last night had not happened until they all went down to breakfast and they were confronted by a large team of Forensic Scientists and Policemen trampling through their home!

Chapter 29.

Sylvia Hendrickson was in a quandary. Just what the hell was she doing? Pietre had not been at the Airport as he had said he would. He had not been in touch at all – so what the devil was she doing in a taxi on the way to the bloody village? She had arrived by train at Thetford and then taken a taxi to Saham Toney. The taxi driver had beamed with delight at the prospect of such a good fare and he was clever enough to realise that the lady sitting in the back of his cab had a lot on her mind and so he refrained from his usual line of banter and concentrated on getting his rather beautiful passenger to her destination. As they drove in silence it occurred to the taxi driver, not for the first time and definitely not for the last, that everyone was busy leading their own lives and he was just a small part of that. He was fascinated by people and he would have loved to have known what was going through the mind of his passenger. Oh! Well! He would never know – that's for sure but it didn't stop him wondering did it?

Sylvia, meanwhile, barely noticed the scenery as she sped towards her destination. She never noticed just how beautiful the countryside was. She had never been to this part of England before but she did not dwell too long on that. She had other, far more pressing, things to concern her.

What had happened to Pietre? She had checked into the Hotel at the airport as Pietre had told her on the telephone. He had booked a reservation in both of their names but where the hell was he? That night she had tried several times to contact Pietre on his cell phone until she remembered Pietre telling her that the signal up at the farmhouse was somewhat erratic to say the least. She could not for the life of her remember the damned name of the cottage but she did remember the name of the pub in the village and so, once she got there, that was where she intended to start her search.

When she had arrived at the pub she had been astonished to discover that it was closed for refurbishment! What the hell was she going to do know? She had stood on the pavement outside the pub for a while wondering just what her next move should be when the door had opened and a man had asked her what she wanted.

Gordon Jarvis had been staggered to learn that the beautiful young woman standing on the street was, in fact, Pieter's girlfriend and he had not hesitated in telling her where the farmhouse was. He had not offered to accompany her there and he hoped she would not think him too rude but he doubted he would ever set foot in that awful place again!

Sylvia had been delighted to find out where the farmhouse was and she was also delighted when Gordon and Mavis, who had by this time come downstairs to investigate, had both insisted that she was to leave her luggage with them at the pub and head straight out to the farmhouse. Sylvia had insisted that Pietre was not to know that she was on her way. She wanted to surprise and, hopefully, to delight him. Oh! My dear! I think it will be you who gets the surprise thought the redoubtable Mavis as she helped her husband with the stranger's luggage. What the hell was happening now she mused? Only time would tell eh?

Sylvia's first sight of the farmhouse was one that would stay in her memory forever. The police cars with their awful flashing lights. The van loaded with all sorts of equipment and people walking around in paper suits and blue plastic shoes over their own footwear. There were people everywhere and things were not helped when the taxi driver said out loud just exactly what she was thinking. "Bloody Hell love, this looks just like one of them murder scenes off the telly doesn't it eh? Oops. Sorry love – bloody thoughtless thing to say wasn't it? Sorry!"

Sylvia paid the man and walked away without saying thank -you- something she later regretted – and walked slowly towards the chaos playing out in front of her astonished gaze. She was stopped almost immediately by a very young policewoman who told her firmly that she was not allowed to go any closer to the farmhouse. This was a crime scene! Did she not realise this? What did she think the tape was there for? Decoration? Sylvia began to explain just exactly who she was when she heard a sound that had her spinning around. Pieter had let out an anguished cry as he had caught sight of her and he ran headlong into her arms as he began to rain kisses on her all the time weeping like a baby. Sylvia had absolutely no idea what the hell was happening and she was more than a little afraid to say the least. She slowly extricated herself from the vice like grip of her boyfriend and held him at arm's length as she tried to fathom out what the hell was going on!

Suddenly an old lady with a beautiful, gentle and kind face stood beside them and slowly and carefully started to peel Pieter's arms away from Sylvia's body all the while making soothing, comforting sounds as they slowly went into the house.

As she sat in the beautiful lounge listening to the story unfolding Sylvia could not quite believe her ears. Surely this sort of thing didn't happen except in third rate movies! Surely?

The introductions had been strained and awkward at first but, gradually, Pieter had calmed down sufficiently to explain to everyone just who this beautiful creature was and also to explain who these amazing people sitting with her were. Everyone was, understandably, subdued but Mavis and Elspeth were making sterling efforts towards being the perfect hostesses. Sylvia smiled inwardly as she took in this surreal scene. Only the English would try to pretend that something dreadful had not happened here the night before. What was it she had heard about the British? Oh! That's right. Something about a stiff upper lip wasn't it? Talking of which Sylvia was only to aware that Maud's husband – Harold wasn't it? – was making a good job of pretending that everything was hunky dory. (That was the phrase wasn't it? The English did have a most peculiar way with words at times didn't they?)

Pieter had tried to explain as best he could the events of the previous night but he had become so distressed that Sylvia thought her own heart would break as well as Pieter's and so it had been decided that ,perhaps, today was not a good day to relive their ordeal. They would have to relive it for the Police as it was and no-one was looking forward to that.

The Officer in charge of the investigation was being brought in from Thetford and would arrive shortly they had been informed by the young Policewoman who Sylvia had met earlier.

As they all waited for the arrival of said Officer Maud was aghast at the prospect of Sylvia having nowhere to stay. The pub was closed for refurbishment because of the recent, awful, events. She insisted that Sylvia was to stay with her and Harold at their little cottage in the village. She had been most adamant and Pietre had put up very little resistance and so, reluctantly, Sylvia had agreed to spend the night there. What they did not realise, however, was just how determined Sylvia Hendrickson could be! She had acceded this time but she was quietly determined that she would find out exactly what had gone on that night and she would do everything she could to make it right for the man sitting forlornly in front of her staring, unseeing, into the void .

Elspeth and Gerry had also insisted that Pieter stay with them in the farmhouse if he could possibly bear it? The Police would need to speak to them all several times throughout the day they thought and so wouldn't it be better for everyone if he was on hand? Don't you think said Elspeth with as much conviction as she could muster? If the truth be known everyone sitting around the lounge would have given anything to not be here and having to go through the trauma of reliving last night. Gordon had walked out against the advice and request of the Officer who was first on the scene. It had been a good job for Gordon that the young, inexperienced, Officer had decided to let Gordon go back to the pub with strict orders to be back here before noon as the Investigating Officer would need to speak to everyone as soon as she arrived! When Harold had heard that the Officer in Charge was a woman he had reacted badly. Maud was both troubled and disappointed to realise that, for all her beloved Husband's advances, he was still having great difficulty in realising that women were more than capable of handling difficult and challenging roles. When this nightmare was over she would make sure she had a quiet word in Harold's ear!

Chapter 30.

D.C.I Miranda Booth was an experienced Officer but she was also more than a little out of her depth and comfort zone. She had painstakingly spoken to everyone individually and she had been astonished and not a little disconcerted by what she had been told! The Forensic team was still hard at work and the crime scene would be out of bounds for a little while longer yet. The moment she was able to enter that room D.C.I Booth wanted, and needed, to see for herself just what had taken place the previous night. She had been in touch with her Superiors and it had been decided that this crime needed to be handled with exceptional care. The last thing anybody wanted was for news of it to get out to the media. What a bloody circus that would be thought Miranda. The media would have a feeding frenzy with all the talk of witchcraft and people hearing voices just before a known criminal with a dubious family history had been blasted to death with a double barrelled shotgun!

Her thoughts were interrupted by the voice of the Senior Forensic Officer telling her that, for now, he had finished his preliminary investigation and she was able to enter the room with strict instructions to stay away from the areas marked out with yellow and black tape.

Miranda picked her way carefully around the crime scene as she tried to piece together in her own head the events of the previous night. She did not believe in ghosts and ghouls but she was absolutely certain of one thing – and that was that something incredible had happened to the people she had been interviewing all that day. She had ascertained some of the details of the so called "vendetta" that had been simmering for centuries according to the Reverend Wellbeloved.

As she continued to make her way slowly around the scene of devastation before her it occurred to her, not for the first time, just how unpredictable life could be! How would anyone suspect that some sort of Satanic Cult was working in this sleepy little village eh? Don't be so ridiculous chided Miranda to herself you've been watching too much T.V – nevertheless D.C.I Miranda Booth was not convinced that she was being ridiculous. She prided herself on her ability to solve any crime that she was given but, right now, she was grateful that this local incident was going to be investigated by her immediate Superiors. She had the distinct feeling that this particular case was going to be memorable and for all the wrong reasons. The sound of her cell phone ringing brought her to her senses and she quickly resumed her role as Lead Detective in the investigation of a suspicious killing here in Saham Toney. "D.C.I Booth speaking. What have you got for me then? "As she listened to her Commanding Officer she nodded and breathed a sigh of relief. She was to hand the case over to Thetford Station and they would take it from there. She might be on the fast track to promotion but this case was going to be trouble – she just knew it!

Sylvia lay, meanwhile, in the guest bedroom at Harold and Maud's rather lovely cottage and wondered just what today held in store for them all. She and Pietre had had precious little time together and Sylvia could not quite shake off the nagging doubt that Pietre was doing his very best to ignore her! What should she do for the best? Should she go quietly and with no fuss back to Sweden and wait to see what happened next? What should she do?

She needed to speak with Pietre – today. She would head back over to the house and confront him. Why did she need to confront Pietre? Such an aggressive turn of phrase to use when thinking about the love of her life but confront him she must if she was to get any sort of answers. With that in mind she dressed and headed to "Haven's Retreat"

Pietre had had an absolutely horrendous night. He had not dared to even contemplate closing his eyes. He knew with awful certainty that his mind would continue to relive the horrors of the previous night and the thought of that was unbearable. What was also unbearable were the voices!

The voices!

What the hell was happening to him now? As if yesterday was not bad enough now he had to contend with all the bloody voices in his head trying to speak at once. Pietre had always had the feeling of Deja-vu but it had never impacted on his life like it was doing now. He had always put things down to coincidence but now he knew that this was no coincidence! He could not explain to himself let alone anybody else what the sensation felt like. He wasn't certain what was going on but he was certain of one thing – and that was that he did not like it! He did not like it at all! The voices, such as they were, didn't really speak to him in words but more in feelings and thoughts. He knew he had heard actual voices the previous evening. Everyone in the room had heard the voices. Today, however, it was different – not better just different. Today the voices clamouring to be heard were all saying variations of the same thing – and that was that if he needed this to be over he must contact Joshua and Flora Bromfield. When he "heard" these names it struck a chord somewhere in the back of his mind. He could hardly think straight at the moment and it had taken him a little while to realise that Joshua and Flora Bromfield were, in fact, his relatives from God knows how long ago. How the hell was he supposed to contact the dead eh? This was getting to be bloody ridiculous. Just a few short months ago he had been in Sweden with both of his Parent's still alive and now look where he was! Stuck in a little village in Norfolk dealing with ghosts, voices and who knew what else.

The Police had informed them all that day that they must not leave the house without permission as they would be needed all day for the ongoing investigation. Gordon Jarvis was to be brought back to the house by an Officer as soon as it was possible but in the meantime they were all stuck in this bloody house! Pietre needed to get out. Quite where he could go he did not know but he just knew he needed to be away from the terrible atmosphere that was pervading everything that he held dear. Almost without realising it Pietre found himself walking in the garden. The beauty and peace of the garden went some little way in relieving the tension he felt. Slowly he began to breathe more easily and his head began to clear. How could something so awful happen in such a beautiful place as this he wondered? The garden was so peaceful and quiet – just what he needed right now. As he sat at the bench in the quietest corner of the garden Pietre became very aware of a change to the voices in his head. Slowly all the clamouring sounds dissipated until he knew, without his realising, that there was only one voice he could "hear".

Flora Bromfield was with him in the garden. Pietre was not frightened – he was somehow comforted by the soothing tone of her voice in his head.

Pietre sat perfectly still in his sanctuary as he "listened" to what Flora had to say. He listened as she related the terrible events that had occurred on her Daughter's wedding day. He listened and he listened.

Later on he could not quantify just exactly what had happened to him that fateful morning but he realised that his "gift" was just that – a gift. He knew that his ancestors had been terribly persecuted and they had suffered enormously for it. He also knew what he must do next. As he stood up and made his way purposefully towards the house Sylvia was watching him and something about his demeanour made her tremble! The haunted look on Pieter's face had been changed to one that she could only describe as being one of complete and utter determination and conviction. What was happening now she wondered as she followed him into the house? Just what did the day and the rest of their lives together hold for them? There was only one way to find out.

When Sylvia caught up with Pietre he was in the kitchen talking to Gerry and Elspeth and he had not realised that she was there. Sylvia knew that he had been discussing something that he didn't want her to hear. That was obvious by the sudden change in the body language of Elspeth as she, quite loudly, said hello to Sylvia and did she want a cup of tea or something?

Pietre swung round at the sound of Elspeth's voice and he quickly excused himself and left her high and dry. Sylvia did not know what to do. She felt that she was, somehow, losing Pietre and she was scared-very scared.

She made her excuses to Gerry and Elspeth and fled the house. She had been told that she could leave the house any time she wanted to as it had been established that she was not connected to the terrible events of the previous night and so she made her way back to Maud and Harold's house where she hoped it would be quiet and she could decide on her future – or more to the point she could decide on her and Pieter's future together. All she knew for certain was that it had been a terrible mistake coming to England and she needed to return to Sweden as soon as she possibly could!

Gerry and Elspeth, meanwhile, were trying to digest what Pieter had started to tell them. He had started to say that he needed to go to the master bedroom as he was certain that something important was hidden there! They had not had the time to ask any further questions before Sylvia had arrived. All they could see for themselves was the expression on Pieter's face and that had been enough for them to realise that it must be very important- very important indeed!

The rest of the morning was uneventful. The Reverend Wellbeloved, Gordon, Oscar and the others were interviewed at length by the Police and were told to wait in the house until further notice. Everyone walked around in a daze with no-one actually talking about the events of last night.

Maud and Elspeth made them all a hearty lunch which everyone, surprisingly, enjoyed and eat. Maybe life would eventually get back to some semblance of normality after all thought Maud as she and Harold did the washing up. The very fact that Harold did the washing up without being cajoled proved to Maud that normality might be some little way off just yet but - small steps eh? Thought Maud as she went into the living room. Sylvia had confessed to her about her concerns and Maud had, hopefully, persuaded her to spend the night in their cottage before making any rash decisions about leaving the country. Pieter is going through a terrible time right now and I know that you are too my Dear Maud had said to Sylvia as she had tried to stem the tears that coursed down the face of the beautiful, confused and frightened girl who had sat beside her in the lounge that very morning. Maud hoped with all her heart that Sylvia would heed her advice and stay for a little longer. She knew just how poorly her beloved Father was and her heart went out to the girl. Everyone was suffering right now weren't they? Maud had made a conscious effort to speak to God that morning. When had she had to make a conscious effort before she wondered? Never. Today, however, she had knelt at the end of her bed and prayed like she had never prayed before. She had prayed for His help in finding a solution to all this tragedy. She had prayed for the strength to see it through and she had prayed that, somehow, some good might come from the tragic and violent things that had happened that night. Finally she had prayed for the soul of Elijah Stump who she felt sure was a decent person deep down. Wasn't everybody really? Deep down? How she hoped that that were true!

After lunch it was Harold who grasped the nettle. "Excuse me everybody. We need to talk. We need to talk about what to do next once the Police have finished."

The silence that followed was excruciating. Oscar finally found his voice. "I know that it is not really my place to say something but I feel that if I don't say something right now I don't think I will ever have the courage again. I truly believe that we must ALL continue with what we tried to do last night. This house is unbearably sad and unhappy and we must do something about that if we can. I know I sound deranged when I say that a house can be unhappy and sad but I really feel that about this place! Sorry!"

As Oscar sat down no-one could look anyone in the eye. Gordon stood up and cleared his throat. "Now, you all know a little about me and you all know that I call a spade a spade so what I am about to say is not easy for me and I hope that I am right about this."

All eyes were on Gordon as he began to slowly pace the floor of the living room.

" I have known this house for longer than all of you, granted it has not been that long but, nevertheless, I do know more about the "feel" of this house than anyone else here. Agreed?"

Everyone in the room nodded.

"Oscar. You are absolutely right in what you say. We must do something for the house and for Gerry, Elspeth and everyone sitting in this room. We have all been affected by recent events and I have had a difficult time in this house ever since I arrived in Norfolk.

I do not believe that this house is "possessed". I do not hold with stupid phrases like that. I do believe, however, that buildings and places have an aura about them."

Gordon could not quite believe that it was his voice saying these things. Anyone who had known him in his previous life in Newcastle would have called for the ambulance and had him carted off to the "funny farm" as soon as look at him! As Gordon thought this he was struck by one particular thing. His "previous life". Exactly. His "previous life". Not his present one with the gorgeous Mavis and these lovely people sitting looking expectantly at him.

"I agree that something needs to be done and it needs to be done soon before I lose my nerve! Agreed?"

Everyone in the room looked at him. No-one spoke for what seemed like an eternity to Gordon.

 Finally Harold broke the silence.

"I think that Gordon is absolutely right in what he has said. I don't hold with the notion of a house being "possessed" either. What I do know, however, is that something needs to be done and done as quickly as possible. What I suggest is that we wait to see what the Police have to say first and then make a decision that all of us are in agreement with. "

Any further discussion was ended as the door to the living room opened and D.C.I Booth entered the room.

"I'm glad that everyone is here as I have something to say."

The atmosphere in the room became, suddenly, electric and D.C.I Booth was very aware that something she didn't quite understand was taking place.

"I have just spoken to my Superior Officer and a decision has been made. It looks from what I can see that the death of Elijah Wood was the result of an incident that occurred during the struggle that took place last night. He was, from all accounts, a man who suffered from some type of mental disorder. He entered the premises and threatened everyone sitting her with a double barrelled shotgun. It has been decided that, pending further investigations, for the time being no further charges will be brought with regard to the death of the said Elijah Wood. If, however, any further information comes to our attention then the case could be re-opened at any time. Do I make myself clear?"

As she surveyed the faces sitting before her D.C.I Booth knew that something other than what appeared to have taken place was going on. Just what that was, exactly, she had no idea. What she did know, without a doubt, was that whatever it was that had happened she doubted that it was all over for the people sitting here in this room.

"The Forensic Team has completed their investigations thus far and I have been authorised to inform you that we will be leaving by the end of today.

 We will, of course, be continuing with our investigations regarding certain aspects of the death of Mr Wood but it seems highly unlikely that any charges will be brought against anyone here in this room for the demise of Mr Wood. I know this might seem a stupid thing to say right now but I hope that this nightmare situation you find yourselves in is over."

Maud Carrington closed the door behind the last of the Police Officers as they left the house and rested her head on the door. This nightmare was not over yet. She wondered if it ever would be for the folks still sitting forlornly in this beautiful house. Her Grandchildren would be back in 2 days. What would they say to them? How would they ever feel safe and happy in this house?

As they sat that night quietly eating the evening meal she and her Mother had prepared Elspeth's thoughts were elsewhere. Just a few short months ago she had had what appeared to be an enviable life in Chelsea. She was married to a handsome, successful, Plastic Surgeon. She had every material thing she could ever have wished for and she had been miserable!

She had been SO miserable.

This house had seemed like the answer to all of their prayers and now looks what had happened. A man had lost his life here in her home. Okay he had been mentally unstable but he had DIED here in her lovely home. What the hell was she supposed to do now? She loved this house. No! She loved this home she had created. She wanted, desperately, to live here all her life. But, how could she now? Would it ever be the same again? The house had a troubled history, that was patently obvious, but the house had also enjoyed many happy times surely? Perhaps it could enjoy happy times again? She hoped so. She really did hope so.

As everyone sat with their after dinner drinks in the living room a real sense of purpose resonated within the walls of "Haven's Retreat". Something could be done; something WOULD be done, to bring happiness and serenity back to this lovely old house. The only thing stopping it was the courage, or lack of it, of the people sitting around the log fire as it crackled away. Would they have the courage to do what was needed?

 The house hoped it would!

Chapter 31.

As the sun burst through the light clouds and enveloped the house with its warmth the atmosphere within the house seemed to improve. No-one had slept much for another night but instead of feeling exhausted everyone felt a strange sort of elation and energy coursing through the house. Pietre had requested that they all meet in the lounge as soon as it was convenient. Gordon had been telephoned and Mavis had informed them that Gordon was already on his way with Oscar and the Reverend. Mavis's voice had been more than a little concerned and it had taken all of Maud's powers of persuasion to convince Mavis that everything was just fine and Gordon would be home before she knew it! Reluctantly Mavis had replaced the receiver on the telephone and looked around her at the state of her home. Everyone had changed so rapidly! Her business had almost ceased to exist. Her beloved Gordon was distant and uncommunicative. She herself had been having nightmares about the whole terrible business and now, to cap it all, Gordon had fled out of the pub at some ridiculous hour saying that he needed some fresh air! What the hell was going on? What the hell was going to happen next?

Gordon had indeed fled the pub as soon as it was light. He needed to escape – not from Mavis – but from his thoughts. He needed some sanctuary and so it was that he found himself standing outside the Church. The last time he had been inside that building was when that maniac had attacked him and the time before that had been the funeral of his dear friend the previous summer. So what the dickens was he doing skulking around outside? Just as he turned away from the Church door he had been surprised to hear it being opened and, suddenly, there stood the Reverend Wellbeloved who had let out a cry of surprise! Almost without realising it Gordon had found himself sitting in a pew and pouring his heart out to Reverend Wellbeloved.

A little over an hour later and a subdued Gordon and the Reverend made their way to "Haven's Retreat". No words passed between them as they collected Oscar, who had stayed in a little Bed and Breakfast place in the village. Oscar felt it inappropriate to ask about the obvious atmosphere in the car and so it was that this assortment of lost souls tentatively knocked on the door of the house.

The scene that they came upon did little to dispel the strained atmosphere. Everyone seemed different somehow! Not negatively different – just different.

Pietre cleared his throat and began to speak.

"Thanks once again to everybody for coming today. The last few days have been truly awful but I hope that we are all still in agreement about what we should do next?"

One by one they all nodded their agreement and so Pietre continued.

"I have spoken to Gerry and Elspeth about what I would like to do today and they have, amazingly, agreed to my bizarre request. Now, Harold and The Reverend Wellbeloved I know that what I am about to say may not sit easy on your consciences.

Yesterday afternoon I was sitting in the garden collecting my thoughts. I was trying to make some sort or sense of it all. As I sat there I became aware of something happening around me. I cannot really explain it to myself let alone anyone else, suffice to say that I truly believe I was in contact with Flora Bromfield who is, in fact, a very distant relation of mine and was the owner of the house when her Daughter was brutally killed by Elijah Woods ancestor."

As he continued speaking Pietre noticed that everyone in the room, including Harold and the Reverend, had not raised any sort of objection to what he was telling them. In fact they were all listening with obvious interest and so that gave Pietre the courage to continue.

"I have asked Gerry and Elspeth if it is okay for me to explore their bedroom for, quite frankly, I don't know what. Flora tried to tell me something about that room but I could not quite comprehend what it was she was telling me. All I do know, however, was that I got the very real sense that this room was extremely important. Like I say I have no idea what significance the master bedroom might have but I feel that I must at least try to find something, does everyone agree? The reason I am asking if you all agree sounds ridiculous now in the morning but last night I had a terrible feeling that if we get this wrong then we could all be in trouble!"

Pietre stopped speaking and held his breath. How idiotic did that sound? What danger could they possibly be in?

Pietre climbed the stairs heading for the master bedroom with absolutely no idea of what he was going to do. He paused before opening the door.

The moment he entered the room he as overwhelmed by a strange mixture of emotions. This room was both equally full of sadness bur also filled with love! Slowly, and inexorably, Pietre was aware that he was not alone in the room. Flora was with him. He sensed, rather than saw, Flora. Pieter felt the need to walk gently and respectfully around the room. As his gaze took in the elegant surroundings Pieter's mind was taken back in time to when the house had been first built. The house was an exciting mixture of love, fun and hope. The house did not feel oppressive in this room. This room, he knew, held the key to all the awful things that had happened here – he was certain of that! Without fully realising it Pietre was drawn to the fireplace that dominated the room. He slowly and gently ran his hands over the surface of the walls around the fireplace; Pietre felt the strangest sensation as he continued to feel around the walls. Flora was desperately trying to tell him something. What was she trying to tell him? It was something about a necklace? What necklace? What do you mean Flora? I don't understand? Pieter's mind was in a whirl and he didn't know what to do next. Suddenly he knew! Suddenly some of it made sense! He raced down the stairs and began calling for Gerry and Elspeth. Within moments the room was filled with everyone in the house. The sound of Pieter's voice had galvanized everyone into action. As everyone stood around not knowing quite what to do the Reverend Wellbeloved found his voice.

Everyone stood transfixed as the Reverend began to quietly chant. Elspeth and Maud began to whimper.

They both wondered if the chanting was the same as the night before and they couldn't have coped with that. As the Reverend continued it became obvious that the chanting was not the same as the previous time. This chant was, somehow, peaceful and calming. Harold and Gordon stood stoically whilst Oscar discreetly crossed himself! He had never been the most religious of men. He liked to work with facts. He liked to know what he was dealing with. He had absolutely no idea where this might lead. What he did know, however, was that he wasn't taking any chances. Gerry silently walked towards the stricken Pietre and gently laid his hand on the poor man's shoulder. This simple act was all it took for Pietre to realise that, maybe, everything would be alright,

"Gerry, Elspeth. I can't explain it to you – or indeed to myself – but I need to see what's behind this fireplace. Do you mind? "

Elspeth was the first to break the dreadful silence.

"Of course Pietre. What do you need us to do?"

"I need to dismantle part of the fireplace. I need to see what's been left behind. I can't explain any more than that. Is that okay?"

Within moments everyone began to move. Maud and Elspeth cleared the fireplace of ornaments. The Reverend and Oscar began to move furniture. Harold was dispatched to find some old dust sheets from the shed whilst Gerry and Gordon collected various hammers etc. that might be useful.

It took a surprising short period of time to unearth the back of the fireplace. This room had hardly been touched in a very long time and the plaster came away very easily. As the dust settled around them everyone held their breath. Just what might they find?

All the time this was going on Pietre stood impassively to one side. The concentration on his face was evident to everyone. He mumbled and muttered to himself the entire time and they all worried about his mental state.

With one simple gesture from Pieter the room went quiet. Slowly and gently Pietre knelt by the side of the fireplace and began to rummage about.

In Pieter's mind he was being guided to a very specific part of the fireplace. He needed to remove just a little more plaster form just above his right shoulder and he would be there!

The gasp that escaped, involuntarily, from Pietre made everyone jump. Maud held on to Harold as though her life depended on it. Elspeth had never been gladder to have her Husband at her side and Gordon looked near to collapse as Pieter's hand touch something hidden in a secret recess built into the fireplace itself.

As Pietre touched the object Flora Bromfield felt an overwhelming sense of relief. Finally, after all this time, she might have some peace. Finally it might be over for them all.

In Pieter's hand he held a small metal box. It had once had a lock and key but, over time, the metal had corroded slightly and so it didn't take much effort to prise the box open.

Inside was a simple but beautiful gold chain with a delicate heart shaped pendant attached to it. On the back was a simple engraving. To Jessica. All our love. Mother and Father. X

Pietre sat on his haunches staring at this simply beautiful thing. Flora stood just beside him looking too. Pietre did not need to look over his shoulder to KNOW that Flora was there. He knew without unquestionable certainty that she was in the room with him. He also realised the significance of what he held in his hand. This was to be a wedding day gift for Jessica on her wedding day. This was a gift that Flora and Joshua never had the chance to give to their beloved child!

As Pietre stood up and looked around him he knew that this nightmare might just be over.

The atmosphere in the room was electric. Harold, Maud, Gerry, Elspeth, Gordon, the Reverend Wellbeloved and Oscar Washington all stood in silence and looked at each other in turn.

"I think I have found what the house has been hiding all these years. I also think that this necklace will help to bring all this to an end. I can't explain exactly how – I just know it."

As everyone left the room they ALL felt a strange sense of calm envelop them all. The house did indeed seem happier. The house seemed to be, finally, at peace with itself.

"Haven's Retreat had held its secret for long enough.

Now, at long last, the house was at peace and today was the start of a new Chapter.

Chapter 32.

SIX MONTHS LATER.

Such a lot had happened in the last six months thought Pietre and Sylvia as they headed back to Norfolk.

The day that the necklace had been discovered things had happened at a remarkable pace. Pietre remembered little about the events in the room that day. What he did remember within uncanny clarity was what he did next.

Pietre had run from the room and headed straight to Harold and Maud's little cottage where he had only just been in time to stop Sylvia from leaving for Sweden. He had tried to explain just what had gone to Sylvia but had kept stopping to kiss her over and over again She could not really take in what he was trying to tell her at first. All she knew was that Pietre was telling her that he loved her and that he was so sorry for putting her through hell and could she forgive him?

They had left for Sweden the very next day because her Father was, by this time, desperately ill. Sylvia and Pietre arrived in Sweden and went straight to her family home. Her Father was barely conscious when they arrived. The morphine he was taking for the pain was dulling his mind and his functions. Sylvia had sobbed uncontrollably as she went on to try to explain that Pietre was her with her and he wanted to ask him a question.

Pietre had looked at the frail dying man lying in front of him and hoped that he would understand what it was he was about to say. When he had finished asking Mr Hendrickson for his permission to marry his only Daughter it had taken an eternity for the old man to react. Sylvia sat on his bed silently weeping and Pietre wondered if he had been too late when slowly and painfully the old man had tried to sit up in bed. The racking cough that emanated from his poor emaciated body was a pitiful sound to hear.

Sven Hendrickson knew he was dying. He knew that he would soon be at peace. As he forced his eyes open he saw his beloved Daughter looking wretched. He saw her adored husband to be standing nervously at his bedside and Sven Hendrickson summoned up the last of his strength to say his final words. "You have my permission and blessing young man. Look after her for me will you? Protect her and keep her safe. Sylvia? Where are you my Darling? I cannot see you. Ah! There you are. Enjoy your life my sweetheart. Don't cry! I am at peace now. "

There was so much more that Sven wanted, and needed, to say to his beloved only child but he did not have the strength left in him and so he lay gently back and went to sleep.

After the death of Sven Hendrickson the Company would be plunged into chaos or so thought the onerous Ludvig Ahlstedt as he made his way to the Boardroom for the emergency meeting that had been called. As he entered the room Ahlstedt had the uneasy feeling that something was wrong. Very wrong!

The meeting had gone horribly wrong. How the hell had that happened? He was CERTAIN that he would be elected as the new Chairman of the Corporation instead he was being escorted for the premises by Security! He had had no idea that his stranglehold on the Company was so tenuous. How could this have happened? Pietre Mortennson and Sylvia had the majority of shares! They had tabled a vote of no confidence in him and his Associates had backed the motion wholeheartedly. He was ruined.

As Pietre and Sylvia watched Ahlstedt as he walked across the car park neither of them felt good about what had just happened. Sylvia was still grieving the loss of her Father and didn't need this stress. Pieter's love for Sylvia grew with every passing day and he looked discreetly at her as she struggled to contain her emotions.

"That man has been a thorn in my side for ever and I for one am glad that he has gone. Aren't you Pietre?"

With that short statement Pietre knew that the Hendrickson Corporation was in safe and strong hands and Pietre simply took hold of Sylvia's hand and led her out of the door to the safety and comfort of their marital home.

They had had a very simple but beautiful ceremony just a few short weeks after Sven's passing. It had been a very emotional day for all concerned.

The marriage had been simple but the honeymoon was going to be very different or his name wasn't Pietre Hendrickson. He just hoped that Sylvia would understand that he needed to return to Norfolk for one final time!

Gerry and Elspeth had, somehow, managed to keep it a secret form everyone that Pietre and Sylvia were coming to stay for a few days on a whistle stop visit before they set off on their official honeymoon. Pietre had told Gerry that he and Sylvia would take at least a month off form the business and would tour the world. "What was the use of having money if you don't know how to spend it eh?" Pietre had said over the telephone and Gerry had agreed with him. What else could he have said?

As he went into the master bedroom once more Gerry could not quite believe what had gone on in there such a short time ago. Elspeth had insisted that the room was to have a complete overhaul. The fireplace had been reinstated and renovated – at some considerable cost mind you! – But Gerry had realised that it was important for Elspeth if they wanted to stay at the farmhouse. Everyone agreed that they wanted to remain at "Haven's Retreat". The house had, indeed, changed. Oh! It looked exactly the same except for the changed in their bedroom but it FELT different. It was a calming, relaxing place to come to at the end of a busy day. The Practice had gone from strength to strength and Elspeth had had one of the barns converted into a Studio for herself.

She had enrolled in a soft furnishings course at the local College and had astounded everyone with her natural talent for fabrics, furnishings and general sense of style. She had created a website and had been both delighted and daunted at the amount of work that was coming her way.

She had had the seal of approval from her so called Chelsea "friends" when she had accepted a commission from one of the "Girls". The sleepless nights and the stress had proved unfounded as this "friend" had only been too delighted to help out her favourite little girl on her new adventure. It must be so lonely and boring stuck out in the sticks my Dear the wretched creature has said over the telephone that day. How Gerry had stopped Elspeth from travelling right there and then to London to strangle the life out of the idiotic woman Gerry never knew – but he had – and the business was going from strength to strength and to top it all one of the new and trendy, home magazines was coming over in the next few weeks to do a feature on the fledgling business.

Gerry smiled to himself as he remembered the panic that Elspeth had gotten into when she first heard this but now he realised that it was just what his delightful, amazing and frustrating wife needed.

As he heard the sounds of the good natured bickering of his two offspring filtering up from downstairs Gerry Carrington thanked his lucky stars that their time in Norfolk had proved such a success.

Thomas was going to cook them a celebratory meal for their guests and Grace was just going to be the most divine and elegant hostess that anyone had ever seen don't you know?

Harold and Maud had settled down in the village. Maud had, thankfully, returned to church and both she and the Reverend Wellbeloved were as thick as thieves. Harold, meanwhile, had discovered that he had enjoyed his helping out with Pietre and the share purchasing and Pietre had very generously said that whenever he needed any more help in that line he would be sure to call him first. Pietre had been true to his word when he discovered another local haulage firm was ripe for a takeover and Harold had been elected onto the board of the new Company as a non-executive member whose sole aim was to keep everyone on their toes and report back to Pietre anything that he thought might concern him.

The Reverend Wellbeloved had been both surprised and overjoyed at his new status within the village as someone you didn't mess with! Quite how that had happened he wasn't quite sure but he wondered if it wasn't something to do with the strange and dark events of the past few months that had had everybody talking? Well, whatever the reason was The Reverend Wellbeloved could only thank God for the upsurge in his Congregation m numbers! God really did move in mysterious ways!

Oscar Washington, meanwhile, was a man on a mission! He had been fascinated by the history and story of "Haven's Retreat" and had been delighted when Pietre has agreed that it would be fascinating to delve further into the chequered history of the house and the village.

He had been more delighted, however, when Pietre and Sylvia had agreed to his idea of writing a book about the house and its history. Oscar had taken early retirement when the latest round of cutbacks had poked its head above the parapet and he now spent every available moment in his research. And he had never been happier!

Pietre and Sylvia's wedding had not been the only one to have happened in recent weeks. Gordon Jarvis had proposed to Mavis Riley just days after all the events that had gone on at the farmhouse and she had said yes!

Gordon had been in contact with his children and had waited anxiously for their reaction. What would they think about him getting married again? They had met Mavis briefly but they had only maintained a relationship of sorts with slightly stilted telephone conversation. Would they approve? Would they even attend? Gordon's fears had proved groundless. His children had been surprised but delighted to know that their Dad had found happiness again. Life was too short for long term regrets and recriminations especially after everything that he had been through recently. As he remembered his children saying that Gordon's mind went back to the immediate aftermath of the death of that poor man. Once the media got wind of it they had swarmed all over the place and it had been impossible to avoid the press for weeks. Thankfully another gory tale had taken over the headlines and slowly the village was returning to some semblance of normality.

The pub was looking spectacular after Mavis had declared that it was about time the old place was dragged into the 21st century. As he surveyed his new found kingdom Gordon raised a glass in silent tribute to his first love and he hoped that she would understand.

Somehow he knew that she would.

As the plane touched down at Heathrow Pietre gripped his Wife's hand. He knew that Sylvia didn't really enjoy flying and he was really pleased that she had agreed to return to Saham Toney one final time. They had spoken at length about the difficulties they had had when they were last there and Sylvia had agreed that it was the best thing for everyone that the next visit would be a different one. A happy one. Sylvia knew just how important it was for Pietre to feel happy again. "Haven's Retreat" would always hold a special place in his heart and she wanted to feel that way too about the place. Maybe this time around it would be different eh?

As she thought this she couldn't help but smile to herself. Pietre thought he was the only one who could keep a secret did he? She had no idea where they were heading for their honeymoon just as Pietre didn't know all of her secrets! She had planned a surprise get together of all of his friends from the summer. Elspeth had only been too delighted to host the event. Everyone had been sworn to secrecy. Sylvia wanted to do this for her Husband so that he would know just how much he is loved and respected by his new friends in Norfolk. People whom Sylvia hoped to count as friends soon enough. The only other little problem she had would be what to tell everyone when they asked her what she wanted to drink. It wasn't the best thing to be drinking – not in her condition anyway!

They arrived late afternoon and Sylvia took advantage of Elspeth's insistence that they need e to rest after travelling all the way from Sweden! Had she guessed? Sylvia hoped not – but a woman's intuition was not something to be dismissed lightly. If she had guessed then Sylvia knew she could rely on Elspeth's discretion.

As Pietre stood in the shower that night he began to sing. He had never been happier than he was right now. The Company was going from strength to strength. He had worried about coming back to "Haven's Retreat" but his worries had proved groundless. The old office had been ripped down and Gerry and Elspeth had restored the hallway to its original size and shape. There was not a trace of the old place to haunt him. He knew, from speaking with Gerry, that this had been a very deliberate act on their part. No-one wanted any sort of physical reminder of the events that had taken place. Their mental reminders were enough – thank you!

The voices had diminished over time. Occasionally he felt the presence of Flora at his side but he was not disturbed by it – on the contrary – he was comforted by it.

He was the last of the line for now. He had a connection with Norfolk that went further than mere blood. He was emotionally connected over the generations and he was glad. He doubted he would ever have the skills that his ancestors had had but he was happy with what skills he did possess. Who would want all of the voices in their heads that the poor unfortunate Elijah had had to deal with eh?

At the thought of poor Elijah Pieter's mood darkened. He had not thought about that man for a while. As he thought of him a new emotion began to form itself. Pity! That man must have gone through hell and back and yet the media vilified him as a mad psychopath who only got what he deserved! Pietre would probably never totally forgive him for what he did and for what he tried to do but a very small part of him realised that, perhaps, he had not been as in charge of his destiny as others might have thought.

As Pietre shook himself dry from the shower so he mentally shook off all thoughts of Elijah Stump, Lizzie Stump and the vendetta that had gone on for generations. Thank God all that's over thought Pietre as he dressed for dinner. He had been both surprised and touched when he had finally been told about the other guests who would be arriving very soon. He was glad that they would all be here to see him give his beautiful bride her new present. He had had the necklace and locket he had found in the fireplace restored. Gerry had instantly agreed to his request that he be allowed to keep it and he would not hear another word about Pietre paying him market value for it .Pietre had therefore made a very generous donation to Gerald and Elspeth's favourite charity – so everyone was pleased!

As the guests arrived and the celebrations began everyone seemed to be enjoyed the delicious food and wine together with the very amusing hostess by the name of Grace who kept regaling them all with tales of the family and all the peculiar things that had happened to them after they had come to live in deepest, darkest Norfolk! Everyone except Sylvia! Every so often she had the strangest feeling. Something was not right! Don't be so foolish she chided herself as Pietre clinked a glass and asked for silence

"Excuse me everyone for interrupting this lovely evening but I just wanted to say a few words." The mock boos and jeers brought a smile to almost everyone's face." I would just like to say how happy I am to see everybody again.

The last time we were all here together the circumstances were very different but I am not going to dwell on that tonight – or indeed – every again! I would just like to say Sylvia that you have made me the happiest person on the planet and I would just like to give you this small token of my love for you."

The sound of everyone cheering drowned out the gasp that escaped from Sylvia. Almost before she saw the necklace Sylvia sensed what it was and she instinctively held her tummy before she rose form the table to accept her beloved Husband's token.

"You look absolutely radiant my Darling. I hope you like it?"

At the word radiant both Maud and Elspeth exchanged discreet glances.

Elsewhere in Thetford another momentous event was also taking place!

Stephanie Davies was in agony. She was screaming blue murder and the harassed midwife was beginning to lose her patience with the young girl in her charge. "Listen Dearie, you ain't the first to have a baby and you won't be the last. Just take deep breaths as I've told you and it will soon be over!"

Stephanie was screaming blue murder for more than one reason.

Don't let him be the Father! Don't let him be the Father – please!

How the hell had she gotten here she wondered – not for the first time. She would never admit to herself let alone to anyone else but she had been a bit to free and easy with her favours recently. She hoped it would be her new Partner's child but she couldn't be sure. What if it was the other bloke's? Which other bloke? There were several contenders. Oh shit! What a mess she was in! Just don't let it be him! What the hell was his name? It had been a one night drunken fumble. Surely it couldn't be his? Could it? As they placed the little girl in her arms Stephanie put off the moment for as long as she could. She knew she must look at the child eventually and so she steeled herself to take a look. The terrible cry of anguish filled the whole ward as the unsmiling face of her new born child looked impassively at her. The child's gaze never left her but, instead of being comforted by it, she knew with terrible certainty that the child was indeed his.

As the infant continued to look at its Mother Elijah Stump's soul began to stir! What was happening? Why did he have this strange feeling that something incredible had just happened.

Elijah had not returned to the farmhouse since the awful events of just a few months ago. He did not need to be reminded of just what he had lost. So why did he feel compelled to return to Saham Toney?

As he wandered unchecked through the hospital Elijah began to hope that what he sensed was actually true.

These idiot people around him had absolutely no idea that a "ghost" was walking amongst them! As he thought of the word "ghost" Elijah let out a maniacal giggle and then was startled to see an older Nurse look around and straight at him! Had she seen him? Did she know what was going on? Elijah forced himself to remain calm. The Nurse had a peculiar look on her face but, at last, she shook her head and left the room.

Elijah Stump walked slowly and deliberately to the cot at the side of the bed. Some idiotic specimen was asleep in the bed at the side of the cot but Elijah wasted no time on her. She was useless he could tell but the child lying awake in the cot was something different. As their eyes met Elijah knew that his hopes had been realised! The infant's eyes never left his as he looked at her. Silently an understanding between them began to be formed. Elijah knew with absolute certainty that this creature before him had the gift! He knew that, in time, he would have his chance for revenge!

Elijah Stump looked at her with undisguised joy.

Flora, meanwhile, had also crept quietly in the room. She had been unnoticed by Elijah and for that Flora was glad. Elijah Stump possessed extraordinary powers of that she had no doubt. What Elijah did not realise was the strength of her own powers but he would no soon enough! Flora would need to keep Pietre informed but she knew that he would do everything he could to stop Elijah from exacting his revenge – but it would not be easy! Quietly flora left the building and went in search of Pietre. She knew exactly what she now needed to finally do!

The story was not over yet ……..!

THE END.

?

Printed in Great Britain
by Amazon